Say You'll Stay
Fortuna Lux

Copyright © 2024 by Fortuna Lux

All rights reserved.

No portion of this book may be reproduced in any form without written permission from the publisher or author, except as permitted by U.S. copyright law.

Contents

Content Warning — V

Dedication — VII

My Writing Playlist — VIII

1. Cara — 1
2. June — 8
3. Cara — 15
4. June — 24
5. Cara — 32
6. June — 41
7. Cara — 49
8. June — 62
9. Cara — 72
10. June — 81
11. Cara — 90
12. June — 99
13. Cara — 108
14. June — 119
15. Cara — 128

16.	June	141
17.	Cara	151
18.	June	164
19.	Cara	176
20.	June	184
21.	Cara	196
About the author		205
Also by		206

Content Warning

Buckle up, my dark darlings because this story is about to take you on one hell of a wild ride.

June and Cara's journey is packed with all the intense, angsty, obsessive goodness you crave. But I also want you to know that this book contains some pretty heavy, disturbing content that may be triggering for some readers.

So let's just get real for a sec - this story delves into some dark territory, including:

Stalking and invasions of privacy (June gets a lil' obsessive, y'all) – Toxic, manipulative relationships – Emotional abuse and control – Explicit sexual content (like, graphic stuff - you've been warned!) – Disturbing mental health struggles – Brief mentions of past physical abuse – Toxic family dynamics – Forced Captivity – Masturbation – Alcohol abuse as a coping mechanism – The taking of sperm without consent –

You get the idea. This isn't fluffy, sparkly romance. It's raw, gritty, and pulls no punches when it comes to the uglier sides of love and the human psyche.

Now, I know a lot of us dark romance readers get off on that kind of intensity. But I also want you to know that I take your mental health seriously. If at any point this story starts to feel like too much, please don't hesitate to put the book down. Your well-being is way more important to me than book sales.

I'm here to tell compelling stories, not traumatize anyone. So listen to that inner voice, and take care of yourself first and foremost, okay? I'll still be here when you're ready.

With that said, strap in, my lovely readers. June and Cara's twisted tale is about to take you on one hell of an emotional roller coaster. Just remember to breathe, take breaks when you need them, and put yourself first.

I'm glad you're here for the ride. Let's do this!

Xoxo,

Your favorite Blue Recluse,

Fortuna Lux

Dedication

The Darkest Prelude - Fortuna Lux

To the souls torn asunder by love's cruel blade,
To the hearts that beat in shadows, unafraid.
This story is your twisted refuge in the night,
A seductive descent for those who crave the darkness and the light.

In these pages, you'll find a love that consumes, destroys, then burns anew,
A tale of broken trust, shattered dreams, and passion that singes through.
So to the lovers who dance with monsters, who bare their scars with pride,
This book is the first step on your dangerously alluring ride.

Cara and June's journey is a mirror of your darkest wants,
A reminder that even the most damaged yearn for romance's haunting taunts.

Their obsession will leave you craving, desperate for more,
As you plummet into the abyss where desire's flames roar.

If you're brave enough to face the tempests of hunger unfurled,
Step into their chaos and let this beginning set your depths awhirl.
For this is merely the prelude to a passage of no return,
Where only the strongest cravings for rapture indefinitely burn.

My Writing Playlist

Songs played on a loop while writing chapter

Dive into the dark, passionate world of "Say You'll Stay" with this carefully curated playlist. Each song reflects the intensity and emotional depth of Cara and June's story, from seductive beginnings to the anguish of betrayal and the hope of redemption; not to mention they were played on loop while writing each chapter. Let these tracks guide you through their unforgettable journey.

Before you start: "Dangerous" by David Guetta ft. Sam Martin
A pulse-pounding introduction to the high-stakes world of "Say You'll Stay."

Chapter 1 Cara:
"Hurt" by Johnny Cash

Chapter 2 June:
"Wicked Games" by The Weeknd

Chapter 3 Cara:
"Broken" by Lovelytheband

Chapter 4 June:
"Possession" by Sarah McLachlan

Chapter 5 Cara:
"Shatter Me" by Lindsey Stirling ft. Lizzy Hale

Chapter 6 June:
"Animal I Have Become" by Three Days Grace

Chapter 7 Cara:
"Breathe Me" by Sia

Chapter 8 June:
"Closer" by Nine Inch Nails

Chapter 9 Cara:
"Hurts Like Hell" by Fleurie

Chapter 10 June:
"I Want You" by Savage Garden

Chapter 11 Cara:
"This Is Goodbye" by Imogen Heap

Chapter 12 June:
"Bring Me to Life" by Evanescence

Chapter 13 Cara:
"Gravity" by Sara Bareilles

Chapter 14 June:
"Losing My Mind" by Stephen Sondheim

Chapter 15 Cara:
"Shattered" by Trading Yesterday

Chapter 16 June:
"Darkside" by Alan Walker & Au/Ra & Tomine Harket

Chapter 17 Cara:
"Someone You Loved" by Lewis Capaldi

Chapter 18 June:
"Haunted" by Beyoncé

Chapter 19 Cara:
"Hallelujah" by Jeff Buckley

Chapter 20 June:
"Madness" by Muse

Chapter 21 Cara:
"Turning Page" by Sleeping At Last

Outro:
As the final notes fade, you've experienced the full spectrum of Cara and June's love story. But there's more to come. With tantalizing bonus scenes on the horizon, keep this playlist close as you delve deeper into the world of "Say You'll Stay."

Happy listening and happy reading—Bonus scenes coming soon!

Bonus Scene June: (Coming Soon)
"Demons" by Imagine Dragons

Bonus Scene Cara: (Coming Soon)
"Saving All My Love for You" by Whitney Houston

Bonus Scene June: (Coming Soon)
"I Would Die for You" by Matt Walters

Bonus Scene: Cara (Coming Soon)
"A Thousand Years" by Christina Perri

Chapter 1
Cara

"Michael was right about you!" The words erupt from my lips, fueled by a surge of hot rage that pounds through my veins. My heart hammers frantically as I propel myself towards the door, every step laced with betrayal.

But the lie tastes bitter on my tongue, a desperate attempt to wound June the way he's wounded me. The sight of me with another man - even if he's entirely fabricated - has sent him into a tailspin, his normally cool demeanor shattered.

And oh, how I relish the sight of it. After all this time as his "bestie", always there but never quite enough, I've finally been granted this rare glimpse behind the Juniper Deveaux facade.

A week ago, I gave him my heart, my trust, my very self. I let down the walls I'd so carefully constructed after the deception and emotional turmoil of my ex, Ray. And June, damn him, had been there through it all - listening to every rant, every bitter argument, offering his steadfast support.

I truly thought he'd be different, that everything would change now that we were really together. But old habits, it seems, die harder than I ever imagined.

My steps falter, and before I know it, June has me pinned against the dull grey wall, his tall frame caging me in. The surface is cold against my back, a jarring contrast to the heat radiating off his body.

My pulse pounds in my ears as his verdant gaze slices through me, sharp and unforgiving. "What did you say, Cara?" His breath, laced with the scent of peppermint and smoke, ghosts over my face. "I dare you to say that shit again!"

The anger surging through me is a living, breathing thing, hot and relentless. I shouldn't have lied, I know that. But after catching him flirting with that vapid socialite right in front of me, the need to hurt him, to make him feel even a fraction of the pain tearing me apart, had been impossible to ignore.

There was no Michael, never has been - Juniper Deveaux has been the only man I wanted, the only one I've ever truly wanted. But I'm not backing down now, no matter how reckless it is to poke the bear.

"I wasn't born twice," I spit out, refusing to break eye contact, "...so I'm not repeating myself."

A cruel sneer twists his lips, a look so foreign on his face that it's almost jarring. In this moment, I don't think he wants to turn me on; no, the shine has left his eyes, pupils dilating as he inhales deeply. His free hand slips between my thighs, fingers searching for proof of my betrayal.

Proof that doesn't exist.

My breath hitches as he shifts the thin fabric aside, dipping into my folds. I hate how my body responds to his touch, even now - a traitorous reaction that only serves to stoke the fire of his possessiveness.

"Is that where you've been, Cara Mia?" His voice is a low, guttural growl, dripping with an ownership that makes my skin crawl. "Offering other men what's mine?"

I should back down, retreat from this confrontation before it spirals any further. But the reckless part of me, the part that's still reeling from his blatant flirtation, refuses to be cowed.

"And what if I did, mama's boy?" I taunt, my voice laced with false bravado. "Would you spank me? Beg me to stay like a good boy?"

Something dangerous flashes in June's eyes, a primal response that sends a shiver of both fear and inexplicable desire down my spine. I've always known how to push his buttons, how to get a rise out of him. But this time, I may have gone too far.

The silence that stretches between us is heavy, suffocating. When June finally speaks, his words are cold, devoid of any warmth. "Get out, Cara. Let me know where you're staying, and I'll send your things."

"June..." His name dies on my lips as his gaze slams into me, a physical force that steals the breath from my lungs.

I want to take it all back, to tell him that he's the only one for me, no matter how long it took me to realize it. That I was stupid, so goddamn stupid, to deny myself his love for so long out of fear. But the pride lodged in my throat refuses to let the words escape.

Instead, I obey, slipping out from under his grasp and heading for the door. June looks at me, his expression a mixture of want and anguish, but he doesn't say anything more. Only his body language, tense and closed off, conveys the finality of this moment.

As I storm out of the apartment, disbelief clings to me, suffocating. "I can't believe you're asking me to leave," I spit out, the words a last, futile attempt to change the outcome. But June's door slams shut, a deafening full stop to our brief saga as more than friends.

The night air bites at my cheeks as I step outside, a stark contrast to the heated intensity of our argument. Wrapping my arms around myself, I try to contain the fury and devastation that threaten to consume me.

How could he let me go so easily, after everything we've been through? After I finally let him in, trusted him with the most fragile parts of myself? The very thought twists in my gut, a physical ache that leaves me reeling.

My feet carry me to the familiar duplex, a place that's always been my refuge. With shaking hands, I push open the door, calling out, "Mama?"

She turns from the kitchen, concern etching her features. "Cara, what happened? You're shaking."

Mama envelops me in a hug, the kind that used to make everything better. "Shh, tell me everything," she murmurs, her voice a soothing balm.

The dam breaks, and I crumble into her arms, spilling every hurtful detail. My body trembles with a cocktail of anger and disbelief. Mama's hands, warm and steadfast, ground me when I feel like I might shatter.

"Why do I feel so cold, Mommy?" My voice is small, lost, a far cry from the fiery defiance that had consumed me moments ago.

"It's shock, baby." She leads me to the couch, wrapping a knitted blanket around my shoulders. "But you're here now, you're safe."

The fabric itches against my skin, a clear reminder that I'm no longer enveloped in June's false promises. "He didn't even fight for us," I whisper, more to myself than to her.

My mother's presence is a silent pillar of strength as she sits beside me. "People show their true colors in the darkest times, Cara. It's not a reflection of you."

I lean into her, allowing the tears to finally fall. The storm of my emotions - the fury, the disbelief, the utter heartbreak - pours out in great, shuddering sobs. Mama's hands, warm and steadfast, ground me when I feel like I might shatter.

Clarity dawns, painful but necessary. "I need to stand on my own, don't I?"

"You've always been stronger than you realized, Cara. It's time you see it too."

Her words, like an anchor in the raging sea of my turmoil, give me the strength to take that first step forward. I may be shattered, but I won't let June's rejection define me.

Just as the first wave of calm begins to wash over me, the sound of laughter breaks through the stillness of the night. Song and Sonya, my twin siblings, burst into the living room, their usual banter filling the space with a much-needed lightness.

Song, with his mischievous grin, throws himself onto the opposite couch, while Sonya, ever the dramatic one, flops down beside him, feigning despair. "Can you believe it? Our boss gave us another popup inspection today!" she exclaims, throwing her hands up in exasperation.

"And guess who's lab aced it again?" Song teases, nudging his sister with his elbow.

My mother gives them a look, a silent signal that speaks volumes, and their laughter fades as they take in my tear-streaked face and the unspoken sorrow hanging thick in the room.

The twins exchange a puzzled look, probably doing that freaky twin thing they do before speaking. "What's going on?" Song asks, his voice a mix of concern and confusion. "Cara, why are you crying?"

Sonya's eyes widen as she takes in my disheveled state. "Oh no, did something happen with June?" Her voice is barely a whisper, tinged with disbelief.

I wipe away a stubborn tear, attempting a weak smile that doesn't reach my eyes. "Yeah, something like that."

The twins exchange a look of shock. Song sits up straighter, his playful demeanor gone. "But you two are like, the dream team. What happened?"

I shake my head, the events too raw, too painful to recount again. My mother, sensing my reluctance, interjects gently. "It's been a tough night for your sister. Let's just say, June and Cara are taking a break."

Sonya's mouth forms a small 'o', and she moves to my side, wrapping an arm around me. "I'm so sorry, Cici."

I nod, a bitter laugh escaping me. "Yeah, me too, sis... me too."

Song leans forward, the typical mischief in his eyes replaced by a rare seriousness. "We can't let him just break our sister's heart... Want me to beat him up?"

A fleeting smile crosses my lips at Song's attempt to lighten the mood, but it fades as quickly as it appeared. "No, Song," I say, my voice devoid of its usual warmth. "Some battles are fought alone, and some... some are simply lost."

Mama's eyes, always so full of wisdom and comfort, search mine, but for once, I find no solace there. She understands, we all do, that some wounds are too deep for platitudes or protective rage.

The twins sit back, their youthful energy dimmed by the weight of my sorrows they're only beginning to understand. They exchange a glance, then go back to a silent conversation I'm no longer privy to.

"What now, Mommy?" My voice is small, lost. But even as I ask the question, the answer reverberates through me - because I have pushed away the source of my warmth, my safety.

June's embrace, his love, is gone thanks to my reckless pride.

Regret washes over me in crushing waves as I recall the cruelty of my taunt about being with another man. What was I thinking? How could I have been so heartless to the person who has loved me unconditionally?

Sobs wrack my body as I remember the light leaving June's eyes, that beautiful forest green turning flinty with hurt and accusation. In that moment, I saw the trust between us fracture, perhaps irreparably. And for what? A fleeting moment of petty vengeance?

"I've ruined everything," I whisper brokenly into the comforting scent of Mama's embrace. "June finally let me in, let me see the depths of his feelings, and I threw it back in his face."

I dissolve into fresh tears, mourning the potential loss of the one person who has meant more to me than anyone else in this world. What if my rash actions cost me the love I've always longed for? What if I can never regain June's trust, never restore the bond I so foolishly severed?

The anguish coils within me, a serpent of regret and fear constricting around my battered heart. All I can do is cling to Mama, letting her reassuring murmurs and soothing caresses pour over me like a salve as I give voice to my agonized sobs.

"I'm so sorry, June," I whisper into the stillness, hoping against hope that somehow, somewhere, he can hear the sincerity in those three words. "Please, please don't give up on me, on us."

Because in that moment, I realize the gravity of my mistake. June isn't just another love, another chapter - he is the other half of my soul. And I fear I've inflicted a wound so deep that no amount of apologies can ever heal it.

Chapter 2
June

The silence of the apartment is suffocating, heavy with the echo of our final fight. I pace like a caged animal, Cara's words still ringing in my ears, a vicious stab to the heart.

"Fucking Michael!" I spit the words out, tasting the bitterness, the betrayal on my tongue. The acrid scent of the bourbon I've been drowning myself in lingers in the air, mingling with the faint traces of Cara's perfume that still cling to the couch.

Seven years of friendship, of stolen glances and secret longing - all shattered in a single moment. The memory of her laughter at the gala, so carefree and genuine, twists like a knife in my gut.

"Will you go to him now, Cara?" I hurl the accusation into the empty room, my voice raw with pain. "Was he there tonight, making you smile in a way I never could?"

I collapse onto the couch, my head in my hands, fingers digging into my scalp as if I could physically remove the images that torment me. "How did it come to this?" I whisper into the void, a tormented plea for answers.

The thought of another man, unworthy and oblivious to her true value, infuriates me. Yet, beneath the anger, there's a gnawing, insidious fear - was I the one who drove her to this? Did my hidden love, once a comforting secret, become a suffocating cage for her?

I pace back and forth in the living room, each step a testament to my growing restlessness. The loft, once a shared haven for Cara and me, now feels like a prison, its spaciousness mocking my inner turmoil. Memories of our time together haunt every corner, every inch saturated with broken promises and lost dreams.

My heart races, a relentless drumbeat against my chest, as anxiety takes hold. This suit, once a symbol of success and normalcy, now feels like chains binding me to a reality I can no longer bear. Without thinking, I start to strip away the layers, a desperate attempt to escape the physical and emotional confines that tighten around me.

But the release is fleeting. The anger that fueled my actions fades, leaving behind a deep, gnawing shame. In the end, as I sit alone amidst the ruins of our bond, I'm left with nothing but the piercing ache of her absence and the haunting aroma of her scent.

Once a source of comfort, Cara's sweet perfume now suffocates me, a cruel reminder of what I've lost. Her essence will forever linger in the vast void of my existence - permanently etched into the fabric of my DNA, and I would have it no other way.

The mere thought instantly strips me of pretense and pride; and a fresh wave of despair overwhelms my senses, dragging me down. I collapse, the weight of my regrets and unfulfilled wishes pulling me to the floor.

Cara's absence is a void that no success…no amount of time, can fill. She is a part of me…always will be, and I can't deny that I've already irrevocably altered the course of my life, making every effort to be hers…because every part of me knows I was born to serve Cara. To love and protect my Cara Mia forever.

My sobs, raw and unguarded, echo through the empty loft, a lonely sound in the vast silence that has taken over our home. I understand the true cost of my choices. Yet despite the pain, despite the relentless chill of her absence, I know in my heart that I wouldn't change a thing.

For in loving her, I discovered a part of myself I never knew existed.

My emotions leaving my body feels heavy, like I'm shattered on the floor of the place we once called ours. The oppressive stillness of the loft bearing witness to my breakdown, a reminder of how alone I truly am now.

There's no escape from this hell of my own making - I reach for another bottle of bourbon, forsaking a glass this time - continuing my futile attempts to drown the taste of betrayal and despair. Each gulp burns…a poor substitute, I'm not even numb. Not even bourbon brings the peace I seek. But I know the truth, even behind the haze of emotion and intoxication.

Cara is the only remedy. Her presence is the cure I desperately crave…to silence the noise in my head.

The room spins, blurring into dark oblivion as I sink deeper into the cold floor, letting the alcohol drag me down into a fitful slumber…praying I'll wake up in the hell I deserve…or the heaven I still dared to dream…putting an end to this fucked-up nightmare.

Sunlight, cruel and unyielding, pierces through the blinds, an unwelcome visitor to my misery. My head pounds in protest, each beat a reminder of the night's torments…just like my empty bed. The shrill ring of my phone pierces the silence, and I flinch, the sound too loud, too jarring.

The caller ID flashes "Mother," and I feel my stomach drop. I considered letting it go to voicemail, but I know better. Elaine Deveaux waits for no one, not even her own son. With a sigh, I answer, bracing myself for the inevitable.

"Juniper," her voice is sharp, cutting through the haze of my misery. "I hope you're ready for the McCleary fundraiser tonight. The family is counting on you to make a good impression."

I close my eyes, the weight of her expectations settling on my shoulders like a physical burden. "Mother, I'm not sure I'm up for it tonight. I—-"

"Nonsense," she interrupts, her tone brooking no argument. "You have a duty to this family, Juniper. It's time you started acting like it."

The unspoken message is clear: my personal life, my happiness, it means nothing in the face of the Deveaux legacy. I'm just a pawn, a piece to be moved and manipulated on the chessboard of high society. And Cara? She was never part of their game.

"I'll be there," I manage, the words tasting like ash in my mouth. "Don't worry, Mother. I know how to play my part."

As the call disconnects, I'm left in a silence that feels even more oppressive than before. The expectations, the duty, the weight of the family name—it's all tied up in the hated name she insists on using. Juniper. A constant reminder that I'll never be free, never truly be myself.

With a heavy heart, I drag myself to the bedroom, each step a Herculean effort. The sight of the perfectly pressed tuxedo waiting for me is a mocking reminder of the charade I'm about to perform.

As I dress, I catch my reflection in the mirror, the man staring back at me a stranger. Gone is the carefree, lovestruck fool who dared to dream of a future with Cara. In his place stands Juniper Deveaux, heir to a legacy of wealth and power, a man trapped by the very privilege that defines him.

The ballroom is a glittering spectacle of opulence and artifice, the air thick with the cloying scent of perfume and the false laughter of the city's elite. I move through the crowd like a ghost, my smile a well-practiced mask, my words carefully chosen to flatter and charm. But inside, I'm screaming, every fiber of my being rebelling against this gilded cage.

And then I see her, the woman my mother has chosen for me. Amethyst Sinclair...she's epitome of everything I'm supposed to want—beauty, breeding, and a family name that rivals my own.

She approaches me with a calculated smile, her eyes appraising, and I feel a wave of revulsion sour my gut. "Juniper, darling," she purrs, her hand coming to rest on my arm like a shackle. "Your mother tells me we're to be great friends."

I swallow the bile rising in my throat, forcing my lips into a semblance of a smile. "Is that so? How... delightful."

But even as I play my role, my mind is filled with thoughts of Cara. The way she laughed, so free and uninhibited, the way her eyes sparkled with warmth and mischief. She was a burst of color in this monochrome world, a breath of life amidst the suffocating pretense.

And now she's gone, driven away by my own failings, my inability to stand up to the crushing weight of expectation.

As Amethyst chatters on, her words meaningless noise, I feel a yawning chasm open up inside me, a void that can never be filled by the trappings of wealth and power. I'm trapped, a prisoner of my own making, forever doomed to play a part that slowly kills me inside.

And in that moment, surrounded by the glittering facades of the elite, I feel myself becoming untethered, a man adrift in a sea of grief.

Cara's presence, her laughter, her warmth - it used to be the anchor that kept me grounded in this superficial world. But now that she's gone, ripped from my embrace by my own foolish actions, I am rudderless.

Her doubt was like a shard of ice piercing my heart. Did she truly believe I could so easily transfer my affections elsewhere after all we've shared?

The thought is insupportable, a vicious agony that leaves me struggling for breath even hours later. This is the cross I've made for myself, and I can only hope that in bearing it, in enduring this punishment of my soul, I can one day attain what a foolish man like me does not deserve - her forgiveness, her love.

"Enough brooding, Juniper," Amethyst's artificially dulcet tones cut through my reverie, her hand like a vise around my arm. "Your mother wishes to make the rounds. We mustn't keep the masses waiting."

I nod woodenly, the facade cracking ever so slightly before I rally, sweeping my features into an inscrutable mask once more.

Play the part, I tell myself. Retreat into the hollowness of this existence and pray the ache numbs before it consumes me entirely.

But with every painted smile, every hollow exchange, a piece of me frays and unravels. Because it is all a sham, an unbearable charade made infinitely more wretched without Cara by my side.

She is the realness, the vibrancy, the part of me that still remembers how to live rather than simply perform.

As the interminable night grinds on, I find myself retreating more frequently to the shadows, gulping down amber-hued oblivion in hopes it will quell the roiling storm within my shattered heart.

Not even the fire of bourbon cannot numb the pervading sense of loss, of unraveling, that leaves me feeling like a stranger in this life I once accepted as my own.

Eventually, blessedly, the gala draws to a close. I make my escape, slipping away from Amethyst's company and my mother's reproachful glares. Out in the street, the night air is a balm, but it cannot cool the fever gripping my soul.

I walk aimlessly, unmindful of direction or destination, a wraith haunting streets that hold no joy for me.

Inevitably, painfully, my steps lead me to the place I've been avoiding - our loft. The place that was meant to be our sanctuary, our home. I pause outside the door, visions of happier times bombarding me with a litany of what I've squandered, what I've lost through my own selfish weakness.

I can almost see Cara there, her smile radiant and inviting as she ushers me inside after a long day.

Almost feel the warmth of her arms as she drew me into her embrace, her presence banishing the weight of the world. Almost taste the blissful contentment that came from sharing this space with her, building a life where love could flourish untainted.

But it is only a specter, a ghost of what can never be rekindled. Because I let my fears rule me, let the expectations of my legacy imprison me within gilded shackles. And in doing so, I severed the bonds that truly set me free - Cara's faith, Cara's love.

Sobs finally break free, wrenching from my soul in great, gulping gasps. I sink to the stoop, unmindful of propriety or appearance, and let the anguish pour forth.

For I have lost the one thing that ever made me feel whole, that ever gave me a purpose beyond wealth and status.

The very best part of myself.

And as the night stretches on in an infinite abyss of loneliness, I am left to gather what tattered remnants of my heart that remain, and somehow, somehow learn to survive without her light to guide me.

Chapter 3
Cara

The sun's gentle warmth filters through the window, a mocking caress that does little to thaw the icy chill settled in my chest. I blink away the remnants of sleep, my hand instinctively reaching for my phone, the harsh glow flaring to life.

An avalanche of notifications greets me, each one a tiny dagger reminding me of the life I've lost. Two weeks have passed in a sluggish, agonizing drip, each day marked by a relentless parade of images across social media - picture after picture of June, his arm wrapped around the waist of his picture-perfect companion.

I scroll through the feed, my heart clenching at the sight of his smile, the way he looks so at ease in this new world he inhabits. They're the epitome of a power couple, their designer outfits and flawless smiles a testament to the life I no longer have a place in.

The ache in my chest intensifies, a throbbing that's become my constant companion these past weeks. I close my eyes, taking a deep breath, willing the pain away, but it's futile. The scent of freshly brewed coffee wafts through the air, mingling with the faint aroma of vanilla and cinnamon from my dresser - a sensory cocktail that does nothing to soothe the turmoil within.

A sudden burst of energy breaks through my melancholic reverie as Sonya bounds into the room, her vibrant presence a welcome intrusion. "Rise and shine, sleepyhead!" she chirps, her voice far too chipper for this ungodly hour.

Sonya perches on the edge of the bed, her bright eyes taking in my disheveled state. I groan, pulling the covers up over my head in a futile attempt to block out the world. "Go away, Sonya. I'm not in the mood."

But my sister is nothing if not persistent. She tugs at the blankets, her laughter filling the room. "Come on, Cara. You can't stay cooped up in here forever. We're going out, and that's final."

I peek out from under the covers, my brow furrowed. "Out? Where?"

Sonya's grin widens, a mischievous glint in her eye. "It's a surprise. But trust me, you'll love it." I hesitate, the temptation to sink back into my cocoon of misery almost overwhelming.

Yet, as I meet Sonya's gaze, I see the love and concern etched into her features. She's been my rock these past weeks, my anchor in the stormy sea of heartbreak. With a reluctant sigh, I sit up, running a hand through my tangled hair. "Fine. But I'm not promising to be good company."

Sonya's smile grows even wider, a silent victory. "That's my girl. Now get your butt out of bed and get ready. We've got a day to seize!"

An hour later, we're settled into a cozy corner of our favorite coffee shop, the rich aroma of freshly ground beans enveloping us like a warm hug. Sonya cradles her oversized mug, her eyes fixed on her phone as she scrolls through her social media feed.

I take a sip of my own coffee, the smooth, slightly bitter flavor gliding over my tongue. It's a small comfort, but one I cling to in the midst of my emotional turmoil. "Ugh, look at this," Sonya says, her nose wrinkling in distaste as she holds out her phone to me.

I lean forward, my stomach clenching at the sight of June and his new girlfriend at some charity gala. They look like they belong on the cover of a magazine, all polished smiles and perfect poise.

"They're really milking this whole 'power couple' thing, aren't they?" Sonya scoffs, her fingers tapping angrily against the screen.

I shrug, trying to appear nonchalant even as my heart twists painfully in my chest. "I guess that's what's expected of them. The Deveaux heir and his socialite girlfriend."

Sonya's gaze softens as she takes in my expression. "Cara, you know that's not what really matters, right? What you and June had... that was real. This?" She gestures to the phone. "This is just a show."

I nod, swallowing past the lump in my throat. "I know. But it doesn't make it hurt any less."

Sonya reaches across the table, her hand finding mine and giving it a reassuring squeeze. "I know, sis. But you're stronger than this. You're going to get through it, and I'll be right here beside you every step of the way."

Her words wrap around me like a warm blanket, a momentary respite from the chill that seems to have taken up permanent residence in my bones. "Thanks, Sonya. I don't know what I'd do without you."

She grins, the sparkle returning to her eyes. "You'd probably be drowning your sorrows in a pint of Ben & Jerry's and binge-watching rom-coms."

I laugh, the sound rusty and foreign to my own ears. "Probably."

As we finish our coffee and head out into the bustling city streets, I feel a flicker of something like hope burning in my chest. It's small, barely an ember, but it's there. A reminder that even in the darkest of times, there's always a glimmer of light.

Back in the sanctuary of my studio, I lose myself in the familiar rhythm of creation. The scratch of pencil against paper, the soft whisper of a brush laden with paint - these are the sounds that fill the space, drowning out the noise of the world outside.

I pour my heart onto the pages, crafting worlds where love always triumphs, and happily-ever-afters are guaranteed. It's a fantasy, I know, but it's one I cling to. A lifeline in the sea of my own shattered dreams.

The hours slip by, the sun dipping below the horizon and casting the room in a soft, golden glow. I lean back, surveying the work spread out before me. It's raw, imperfect, but it's mine. A tangible expression of the emotions swirling inside me.

My phone buzzes, breaking the spell. I glance at the screen, my heart skipping a beat as I see the notification. An email from one of the animation studios I applied to, the one I've been dreaming of working for since I first picked up a pencil.

With trembling fingers, I open the message, my eyes scanning the words. "Dear Ms. Briers, we were impressed by your portfolio and would like to invite you for an interview…"

I read it again, hardly daring to believe it. They want to meet me. They think I have potential.

A grin spreads across my face, the first genuine smile I've felt in weeks. I jump to my feet, a burst of energy coursing through my veins. "Sonya!" I yell, my voice echoing through the apartment. "Sonya, you won't believe it!"

She appears in the doorway, her eyes wide with concern. "What is it? What happened?"

I thrust my phone into her hands, unable to contain my excitement. "Look! The animation studio, they want to interview me!"

Sonya's face splits into a grin, her eyes shining with pride. "Cara, that's amazing! I knew they'd see how talented you are."

She pulls me into a hug, her laughter mixing with mine as we dance around the room. For a moment, everything else fades away - the pain, the heartbreak, the constant ache of missing June. In this moment, there's only joy, pure and unbridled.

But even as I revel in this victory, a small part of me can't help but wonder what June would think. Would he be proud of me? Would he see this as a sign that I'm moving on, leaving him behind?

His name is a sigh, a lament for what once was and what now seemed an impossible dream. "June..."

"Is an idiot, Cara. You deserve so much better...try to forget about him," Sonya squeezes my hand, her voice fierce, protective. "Besides, you're my sister, the biracial Picasso and a baddie; you can do way better than Juniper."

I nod, clinging to her words, yet doubt still nags at my unsteady confidence. Had I been so easy to replace? Was our connection so superficial that it could be severed without a second thought?

I push the thoughts away, refusing to let them taint this moment. This is about me, about my dreams and my future. June made his choice, and now I'm making mine.

As the day of the interview arrives, I'm a bundle of nerves. I change my outfit three times, second-guessing every choice. Sonya finally intervenes, plucking a simple blue dress from my closet. "This one. It brings out your eyes."

I take a deep breath, smoothing my hands over the soft fabric. "Okay. I can do this."

Sonya grins, squeezing my shoulders. "Damn right you can. You're Cara Briers, artist extraordinaire. You've got this."

Her words echo in my mind as I make my way to the studio, my portfolio clutched tightly to my chest. The building looms before me, all sleek lines and gleaming glass. I take a moment to collect myself, inhaling deeply and letting the cool, crisp air fill my lungs.

The interview is a whirlwind of passionate discussions and probing questions. I speak from the heart, my love for my craft evident in every word. As we wrap up, one of the interviewers leans forward, a curious glint in her eye.

"I have to ask, Cara. How did you manage to get a recommendation from Elaine Deveaux? She's notoriously hard to impress."

My heart stutters in my chest, my mind reeling. Elaine Deveaux? June's mother? Why would she recommend me?

I clear my throat, trying to gather my thoughts. "I... I honestly had no idea. I applied on my own merit. I didn't even know she was aware of my work."

The interviewer nods, a knowing smile tugging at her lips. "Well, consider yourself lucky. A recommendation from Elaine Deveaux is like a golden ticket in this industry. We're thrilled to have you on board, Cara."

As I leave the studio, my head is spinning. June's mother, the woman who had always made it clear that I wasn't good enough for her son, had recommended me. It doesn't make sense.

But as I step out into the sunlight, a realization dawns on me. Maybe it doesn't have to make sense. Maybe this is a sign that I'm on the right path, that I'm meant for something more than being June's girl.

I think back to all the times June and I had talked about the future, about our hopes and dreams. He had always believed in me, even when I doubted myself.

"You're going to change the world, Cara," he'd say, his eyes shining with conviction. "I can't wait to see it happen."

The memory brings a bittersweet smile to my face. June may not be by my side anymore, but his belief in me, his support - it's still a part of me. It's woven into the fabric of who I am.

As I make my way back home, I feel a new sense of direction settling over me. I may have lost June, but I've found something else - faith in myself and my abilities.

I pull out my phone, my fingers flying over the screen as I type out a message to Sonya. "Guess who's the newest member of the Dragonfly Animation team?"

Her response is immediate, a flurry of celebratory emojis and exclamation points. "YES! That's my girl! We're celebrating tonight, no excuses."

I grin, a laugh bubbling up from deep inside me. "Wouldn't dream of missing it. First round's on you."

As I slip my phone back into my pocket, I catch a glimpse of my reflection in a store window. The girl looking back at me is different from the one who woke up this morning. Her eyes are brighter, her smile more genuine. She's a girl who knows her own worth, who's ready to take on the world.

"Watch out, world," I whisper, my grin widening. "Cara Briers is just getting started."

And with that, I turn towards home, towards my future. Because I know now, with unshakable certainty, that I have the power to create my own masterpiece. One brushstroke at a time.

As I make my way back home, the weight of June's absence settles over me like a heavy cloak. Every step I take feels like I'm dragging a piece of my heart behind me, a trail of shattered dreams and unspoken longings.

I can't stop thinking about him - the way his eyes would light up when he talked about our future, the gentle way he'd tuck a stray lock of hair behind my ear. Those little moments, the ones I once took for granted, now loom large in my mind, taunting me with all that I've lost.

Entering my apartment feels like stepping into a void, the silence a constant reminder of his absence. I make my way to the bedroom, my fingers tracing the familiar contours of the furniture, searching for any lingering trace of June's comforting presence.

My eyes land on the framed photo on the dresser, the one of us laughing together at some long-forgotten party. The image is a bittersweet balm to my aching heart, a snapshot of a time when our love felt indestructible, unbreakable.

I sink down onto the bed, the mattress still faintly imbued with his scent, and I can't hold back the tears any longer. They flow freely, a testament to the depth of my grief, the ache of a love that was so cruelly severed.

Reaching for my phone, I find myself scrolling through our old text messages, each word a dagger to my soul. The casual banter, the soft endearments - they're a cruel reminder of all that we once shared.

My thumb hovers over the screen, the urge to reach out to him, to hear his voice, nearly overwhelming. But fear and pride war within me, a constant battle that keeps me from taking that final step.

What if he's moved on? What if I'm only opening myself up to more heartbreak? The what-ifs swirl in my mind, paralyzing me, keeping me from taking that leap of faith.

And yet, a part of me can't help but wonder - what if he still cares? What if, like me, he's struggling to find his way back to the connection we once shared?

The thought sends a flutter of hope through my chest, a fragile flame in the darkness. With a deep breath, I begin to type, my fingers trembling as I compose a message.

"June... I... I got a job offer today. The animation studio, the one I've been dreaming of. They want me to start next month. I just thought you should know."

My thumb hovers over the send button, my heart pounding in my ears. This is it, the moment of truth. Do I take the risk, open myself up to the possibility of reconciliation? Or do I play it safe, protect the shattered pieces of my heart?

In the end, the choice is taken from me as I hear the front door open, Sonya's cheerful voice calling out. With a resigned sigh, I delete the draft, the words disappearing into the ether, just like the fading hope in my chest.

"Maybe another time," I whisper to the empty room, the ghost of June's name lingering on my lips.

For now, I'll focus on my future, on the opportunities that are finally starting to unfold. But a part of me will always be waiting, hoping that one day, June will find his way back to me.

Until then, I'll carry the weight of our shared history, the memories that both comfort and haunt me. Because despite the pain, despite the uncertainty that lies ahead, I know that the love we once shared will always be a part of who I am.

Chapter 4
June

The clinking of silverware against porcelain and the muted chatter of the restaurant's patrons create a symphony of feigned normalcy. I sit across from Amethyst, her perfectly manicured fingers toying with the stem of her wine glass as she regales me with tales of her latest shopping spree.

"And then, I found the most exquisite Chanel clutch. It was like it was made for me, June," she gushes, her eyes sparkling with a materialistic glee that I can't quite bring myself to share.

A wave of revulsion sours my gut as I look at Amethyst, her calculated grace and practiced charm a far cry from the vibrant, genuine warmth I crave. I force a smile that feels more like a grimace. "That's great, Amethyst. I'm glad you found something you like."

She leans forward, her hand coming to rest on mine, the contact cold and artificial. "You know, June, I was thinking maybe we could go shopping together sometime. I'd love to help you pick out some new pieces for your wardrobe."

I resist the urge to pull my hand away, instead offering a noncommittal hum. "Maybe. I've been pretty busy lately with work and everything."

Amethyst pouts, her perfectly painted lips forming a moue of disappointment. "You're always so busy, June. I feel like I hardly see you anymore."

I sigh, the weight of my family's expectations and my own inner turmoil pressing down on me like a physical force. "I know, Amethyst. I'm sorry. It's just...a lot is going on."

She nods, her expression softening into one of feigned sympathy. "I understand, June. But remember, I'm here for you. Whenever you need me."

The lie tastes bitter on my tongue as I force another smile, the muscles in my face aching with the effort. "Thanks, Amethyst. That means a lot."

We lapse into silence, the clinking of silverware and the muted chatter of the restaurant filling the space between us. I feel like I'm suffocating, trapped in a life that doesn't fit, playing a role that I never asked for.

And then, like a bolt of lightning splitting the sky, I hear it - a laugh, bright and familiar, cutting through the din of the restaurant like a beacon in the darkness. My head snaps up, my eyes scanning the room, searching for the source of that sound.

There she is. Cara. She's sitting at a table across the room, her head thrown back in laughter, her face alight with a joy that I haven't seen in months. But she's not alone. There's a man sitting beside her, his head bent close to hers, a hand resting on her arm in a gesture that speaks of intimacy and familiarity.

I feel like I've been punched in the gut, the air rushing out of my lungs in a painful whoosh. Jealousy, hot and bitter, rises up in my throat, choking me. Is this him? The man she left me for? The reason she walked away from everything we had, everything we could have been?

Amethyst's voice fades into the background, a distant buzz drowned out by the roaring in my ears. I stand abruptly, my chair scraping against the floor with a jarring screech. Amethyst looks up at me, her eyes wide with surprise.

"June? What's wrong?" she asks, her voice laced with concern. I shake my head, unable to form words past the lump in my throat.

Propelled by a force I can't control, I stand, my heart pounding as I make my way across the room. They're laughing now, shared amusement lighting up their faces in a way that tears at the very fabric of my composure. I used to be the one making her laugh like that.

"Cara," her name leaves my lips before I can think better of it, cutting through the low hum of restaurant noise, loaded with weeks of silence, pain, and misunderstanding.

As I approach their table, Cara looks up, her laughter dying on her lips as her eyes meet mine. I see the shock register on her face, followed quickly by something else - something guarded, something pained.

"Cara," I say, my voice rough with emotion. "Can we talk?"

She hesitates, her eyes darting to the man beside her. He looks up at me, confusion etched across his face. "Who are you?" he asks, his tone polite but wary.

"I'm Juniper Deveaux," I reply, my gaze never leaving Cara's face. The Deveaux name feels like a shackle, a cruel reminder of the expectations that have torn us apart. "Cara's... companion."

The word tastes like ash on my tongue, a bitter reminder of everything we once were, everything we'll never be again. I hate having to invoke my family's weight, to flaunt the privilege that has suffocated me, when all I want is to be seen as simply June - the man who loves her beyond measure.

Cara stands, her movements stiff and awkward. "Juniper, I don't think this is a good idea. I'm here with someone."

I nod, swallowing past the lump in my throat. "I know. But please, Cara. Just a few minutes. That's all I'm asking."

She hesitates, her eyes searching mine. For a moment, I think she's going to refuse, to turn away and leave me standing there, alone and humiliated by the very name I've tried to shed. But then she nods, her shoulders sagging in resignation.

"Fine. A few minutes."

She turns to the man beside her, murmuring something I can't hear. He nods, his expression still wary, but he doesn't protest as Cara steps away from the table, leading me towards a quiet corner of the restaurant.

As we walk, I can feel the weight of Amethyst's gaze on my back, boring into me like a physical force. But I don't turn around. I can't. Not when Cara is so close, not when I finally have a chance to talk to her, to try to understand what went wrong between us.

We come to a stop in a secluded alcove, the noise of the restaurant fading into the background. Cara turns to face me, her arms crossed over her chest, her expression guarded.

"What do you want, June?" she asks, her voice tired and strained.

I take a deep breath, trying to gather my thoughts. There's so much I want to say, so much I need to know. But in the end, only one question matters.

"Why, Cara? Is that Michael..." I ask, my voice barely above a whisper. "The man you left me for?"

She closes her eyes, her shoulders sagging as if under a great weight. When she speaks, her voice is soft and sad.

"June, I didn't leave you. You pushed me away."

I open my mouth to protest, but she holds up a hand, cutting me off.

"No, let me finish. You pushed me away with your secrets, with your lies. I couldn't do it anymore, June. I couldn't be with someone who couldn't trust me, who couldn't let me in."

I feel like I've been slapped, her words hitting me like a physical blow. "Cara, I never meant to hurt you. I was trying to protect you."

She laughs, a bitter, humorless sound. "Protect me? From what, June? From the truth? From the reality of who you are, of what your family is?"

I shake my head, desperate to make her understand. "No, Cara. I was trying to protect you from my mother, from the expectations that come with being a Deveaux. I didn't want you to get caught up in all of that."

She sighs, her shoulders slumping in defeat. "June, I was already caught up in it. From the moment I met you, I was caught up in your world. But you never trusted me enough to let me in, to let me help you carry that burden."

I reach out, my hand hovering in the space between us. "Cara, I'm sorry. I never meant to make you feel like I didn't trust you. I do trust you, more than anyone."

She steps back, shaking her head. "It's too late, June. I can't go back to the way things were. I deserve better than that. I deserve someone who will be honest with me, who will let me in."

I feel like I'm drowning, the weight of her words pulling me under. "Cara, please. Don't do this. Don't give up on us."

She smiles, a sad, wistful curve of her lips. "There is no us anymore, June. There hasn't been for a long time."

She turns to walk away, but I reach out, my fingers closing around her wrist. "Cara, wait. Please."

She pauses, her back to me, her shoulders tense. "What do you want from me, June?"

I swallow past the lump in my throat, my voice rough with emotion. "I want another chance, Cara. I want to make things right between us. I want to be the man you deserve."

She turns to face me, her eyes searching mine. For a moment, I think I see a flicker of something in their depths - hope, maybe. Or longing. But then it's gone, replaced by a steely resolve.

"I'm sorry, June. But I can't give you what you want. Not anymore. Besides, don't you have a new girlfriend now?"

She pulls her wrist from my grasp, her touch lingering for a moment before she steps back, putting distance between us.

"Goodbye, June."

And then she's gone, walking away from me, back to the man who has taken my place at her side. I watch her go, my heart breaking with every step she takes.

I don't know how long I stand there, staring at the space where she once stood. Minutes, hours, it all blends together in a haze of pain and regret. Eventually, I feel a hand on my arm, gentle but insistent.

"June? Are you okay?"

She leaves with a grace that makes my heart clench, her companion following, a hand lightly touching her back - a casual gesture that sends waves of anger and hurt crashing through me.

Cara's words echo in my mind, a mantra of missed chances and miscommunications. I'm spiraling, caught in a vortex of what-ifs and could-have-beens. The memories...our history, clash violently with the present, a chaotic symphony of emotions that leaves me staggering under its weight.

I turn to see Amethyst standing beside me, her eyes wide with concern. I shake my head, unable to form words past the lump in my throat.

"Come on," she says, her voice soft and coaxing. "Let's get out of here."

I let her lead me out of the restaurant, my feet moving on autopilot. As we step out into the night, the cool air hits me like a slap in the face, jolting me out of my stupor.

"Amethyst, I'm sorry," I say, my voice rough and raw. "I shouldn't have left you like that."

She shakes her head, her hand tightening on my arm. "It's okay, June. I understand."

But she doesn't understand. She can't. Because she doesn't know the truth about Cara, about the history we share, about the love that still burns in my heart, even now, even after everything.

As we walk down the street, the city lights blurring together in a haze of neon and shadow, I feel like I'm walking through a dream. A nightmare, really. One where the woman I love is gone, and I'm left with nothing but the bitter taste of regret and the knowledge that I have no one to blame but myself.

I glance over at Amethyst, her profile outlined in the glow of the streetlights. She's beautiful, in a cold, untouchable way. The kind of beauty that belongs on a pedestal, not in the messy, imperfect reality of life.

And that's the problem, really. Amethyst is a dream, a fantasy. But Cara? Cara is real. She's flesh and blood and laughter and tears. She's the one who knows me, really knows me, in a way that no one else ever has.

And I let her go. I pushed her away with my secrets and my lies, with my inability to let her in, to trust her with the truth of who I am.

As we walk, the city lights fading into the distance, I make a silent vow to myself. I will find a way to win Cara back. I will earn her trust, and her forgiveness. I will be the man she deserves, the man I know I can be.

But first, I need to uncover the truth about the man who has taken my place. I need to know who he is. What he means to Cara...I need to understand what I'm up against.

And then, I will fight for her. I will fight for us. Because in the end, that's all that matters. Cara is all that matters.

And I will do whatever it takes to make her mine again.

Chapter 5
Cara

I step into the backyard, and it almost feels like Mother Nature herself is playing with my head too; the sun is scorching hot against my skin, yet the air is heavy with the scent of incoming rain here in my little garden - my new haven and prison all in one.

It's my favorite blend of floral sweetness and earthy undertones, but even now it does little to soothe the restless energy thrumming through my veins. The hibiscus, with its vibrant blooms, stands tall and proud, while the bamboo, stoic and serene, weaves a lattice of shadows beneath its delicate leaves.

But I can't indulge in their beauty, not today. Even here, in this riot of color, a canvas splashed with vibrant hues, I pray will ease the dullness that seems to have seeped into my very bones in my isolation. This is my new kingdom, a tiny patch of green that now serves as my refuge.

"Just you and me, kid," I mutter to myself, the words catching on the lump in my throat.

The oppressive warmth and the promise of a storm only serve to mirror the turmoil brewing within. I sink onto the weathered bench, my fingers tracing patterns in the damp soil, as I try to find solace in the familiar rhythms of nature.

Yet the hibiscus and bamboo, for all their resilience, and cloying sweetness...mocks the churning restlessness clawing at my veins. Constantly reminding me of what I've lost; the one who left me behind.

Juniper Deveaux—the man who broke my heart; the very essence of my longing and delusional desire—He's like a fragrance that clings to memories, refusing to fade, even as time marches on.

I pause at the clothesline, my fingers brushing against the damp fabric, a tactile reminder of the simple rituals that now shape my days. It's been weeks since that fateful night, but the ache in my chest is as fresh as ever.

Why can't I stop missing you? You were never good for my heart to begin with...but somehow I still can't let you go.

My mind's so fucked I can't even create, constantly looking over my shoulder. Strange messages at my door. Even the annex, once my beacon of hope and creativity, now feels like just another cage, its walls pressing in on me with each passing day.

I try to lose myself in the mundane task of laundry, but my mind refuses to settle, constantly circling back to the unanswered questions that plague me. The missing underwear, a seemingly trivial detail, takes on a sinister cast in the light of my growing paranoia.

"Get it together, Cara," I scold myself, my voice harsher than intended. "It's just a pair of panties, not a fucking conspiracy."

But the prickling unease persists, phantom eyes needling my skin. I'm flayed open, laid bare, a quivering nerve forever exposed.

Frustration a roiling tide, I abandon the farce of productivity, retreating inside. But even here, the past lurks, lying in ambush.

Art, my steadfast companion, betrays me now. Pencils leaden in my hand, sketches lifeless and uninspired. The blank page sneers, a mirror of the emptiness clawing at my gut.

Snarling, I banish the sketchbook, grasping for the mindless oblivion of social media. But even there, his face assails me. Each post a twist of the knife lodged in my chest, a fresh laceration to my mangled soul.

Salvation comes in the chirp of an incoming FaceTime, Sonya and Song's fractured grins dispelling the shadows, if only for a heartbeat. "Hey, troublemakers," I force past numb lips. "To what do I owe the pleasure?"

"Can't a couple of loving siblings check in on their favorite sister?" Sonya teases, her grin wide and infectious.

"I'm your only sister, dumbass," I shoot back, the banter familiar and comforting.

"Details, details," Song chimes in, his eyes crinkling with mirth.

Sonya's voice is molten sunshine, her brash concern a welcome scald. Banter flows, the parry and thrust of sibling love a tenuous lifeline.

"But seriously, Care-bear, how are you holding up?" The concern in his voice cracks something open inside me, and suddenly, the tears I've been holding back for days come rushing to the surface.

"I'm drowning," I confess, the words blood and broken glass on my tongue.

Sonya's face softens, her usual teasing veneer falling away. "Oh, honey," she murmurs, her eyes shining with sympathy. "I wish I could give you a hug right now."

"Me too," I choke out, swiping at the tears that now flow freely down my cheeks. "I just... I feel so lost, you know? Like I don't even know who I am anymore without him."

"Hey, none of that," Song says firmly, his brow furrowing with determination. "You are Cara Briers, the most badass artist and sister in the whole damn world. No man, not even June Deveaux, can take that away from you."

I let out a watery laugh, the fierceness of his love a balm to my battered soul. "Thanks, Songbird," I sniffle, using the childhood nickname that always makes him groan. "I needed that."

"Anytime, sis," he replies, his smile soft and understanding. "We're here for you, always."

Promises of a sibling night, a port in this endless storm, then silence rushes back in, thick and cloying.

The demons circle, their clawed fingers scraping against the fragile walls of my psyche, drawn to the raw, bleeding wounds of my misery. Their shadows dance in the corners of my vision, taunting whispers that burrow into the deepest recesses of my mind.

"You're alone," they hiss, their voices a cacophony of twisted truths. "Abandoned. Unworthy. He's moved on, left you to drown in your sorrows."

I squeeze my eyes shut, willing the phantoms to retreat, but their icy tendrils only tighten their grip. Panic rises like bile in my throat, choking off my breath as I struggle to hold back the tide of their relentless onslaught.

Then, a knock - sudden, insistent, jarring - shatters the brittle silence, and a wild, desperate hope surges through me, flooding my veins with adrenaline.

June—returned to piece me back together, to banish the demons that have taken root in my shattered heart.

I wrench open the door, every nerve ending alight with anticipation. But it's not June standing there, not the man I've ached for with every fiber of my being.

It's just Alex standing there. Worry etched into the lines of our friend's face, brow creased with concern...

And the bubble of hope bursts, leaving behind only a dull, throbbing ache. The demons howl in triumph, sensing my vulnerability, their claws scrabbling at the last vestiges of my composure.

"Hey, stranger," Alex says, their voice soft and cautious. "Can I come in?"

I teeter on the precipice, torn between the desire to retreat; pull away to deal with my depression alone, and the steadying pull of Alex's concerned gaze.

The demons sense my indecision, their laughter echoing in the hollows of my chest, taunting me with the shame of my own wishful thinking.

But something in the way Alex holds my gaze, unwavering and sure, pushes back the shadows, and I find myself stepping aside, the words scraping past the lump in my throat. "Yeah. Of course."

We settle, an island of carefully maintained distance amid the detritus of my unraveling. Their nervous energy palpable, a mirror of my own barely leashed turmoil.

"I saw June. He's a wreck, Cara."

His name, a dagger between my ribs, stealing breath and reason alike. "He made his choice," I choke out, each word ashes on my tongue. "He let me go."

Alex's touch anchors me, their voice a lifeline thrown into the maelstrom. "It's not that simple. He's lost too, Cara."

Bitter mirth burbles up, venom and vitriol. "Funny way of showing it, parading around with his new accessory."

"People lash out when they're hurt. They run from the pain, even if it means losing what matters most."

Their wisdom is a lance to my festering wounds, drawing poison to the surface. "When did you get so wise?" I rasp, unshed tears clogging my throat.

"Somewhere between tequila and regret," they quip, gallows humor falling flat.

Silence stretches, a gulf of shared history and unspoken understanding. "I'm adrift, Alex. Cutting him out feels like carving away pieces of myself."

Steady pressure on my knee, a tether to a world gone mad. "Take it one breath at a time, Cara. You don't need all the answers now."

The tears fall unchecked, salt and sorrow. "What if the pain never stops?"

"Then you learn to carry it. To build a life around the hurt, brick by brick. To risk your heart again, even when it feels like the end of everything."

Their words wash over me, a temporary balm to my fractured psyche. "Thank you. For being my port in the storm."

"Anytime, babe. Dragging your ass out of the pit of despair is what I do best."

Laughter, rusty and unfamiliar, a chink in my armor of anguish. Slowly, painstakingly, the day inches forward. Tears and laughter, memory and revelation, all bleeding together in a twisted tapestry of shared history.

As the sun dips below the horizon, painting the world in shades of bruise and apology, a fragile flicker of hope alights in my chest. The barest ember, stubbornly clinging to life amidst the ashes of my scorched heart.

Alex pulls me close, their embrace a promise and a prayer. "You're going to be okay, Cara. Not today, maybe not tomorrow. But someday. I promise."

I breathe deep, pulling jasmine and agony into lungs too used to sobbing. In this moment, balanced on the knife's edge of despair and determination, I make a silent vow.

No matter what fresh hell awaits, no matter how long I must crawl through the wreckage of my life, I will endure. I will claw my way back to the woman I once was, the woman I could still become.

Even if it means learning to live with the specter of June's memory, a phantom limb forever aching for his touch. Even if it means relearning how to trust, how to love, one stumbling step at a time.

Still, the demons' cruel laughter boo and taunt, even as Alex's comforting embrace anchors me to the present.

And the respite is fleeting, for as I pull back, a sudden shift in the air sets my nerves on edge.

"Did you...did you hear that?" I glance around warily, half-expecting the demons to materialize before my eyes.

Alex furrows their brow, scanning the room. "Hear what?"

I shake my head, a shiver racing down my spine. "Nothing, I guess. I'm just...on edge, that's all."

As if summoned by my unease, a sharp rap at the door makes me jump. Alex squeezes my hand reassuringly before rising to answer it. I hold my breath, heart pounding, as they return with a plain, unmarked envelope.

"This was just left on your doorstep," they say, handing it to me with a concerned expression.

My fingers tremble as I tear it open, the weight of the paper sending a prickle of fear down my spine. A single sheet falls into my lap, the words scrawled in an untidy scrawl that sets my teeth on edge.

"You should be too busy to chase after boys. Won't you be a good girl? Draw your little cartoons...or else."

The threat hangs in the air, a physical presence that steals all rational thought. I glance up at Alex, seeing the dawning realization in their eyes.

"Cara, is this...?"

I nod mutely, the memory of a previous encounter flooding back. "A few weeks ago, I got another one. Vague, just like this. I tried to report it, but the police..." I let out a humorless laugh, "they didn't take it seriously."

Alex's face hardens, their protective instincts flaring to life. "That's it, we're calling the cops. This isn't a joke, Cara."

I reach out, grasping their sleeve. "No, Alex, please. They won't do anything. They'll just tell me I'm overreacting, that there's no real threat."

"But Cara, you can't just ignore this!" Their voice rises in frustration, laced with genuine concern.

I squeeze Alex's hand, willing them to understand. "I know, but trust me, it'll only make things worse. I...I don't know what to do, but I can't let the police get involved. Not yet—they'll think I'm crazy."

Alex searches my face, before looking away. I know my friend doesn't like any of this, but what else can I do?

Finally, Alex nods, pulling me into another tight embrace. "Okay, Cara. Okay. But promise me you'll tell me immediately if anything else happens, understand?"

I nod against their shoulder, the weight of the threat and my own helplessness threatening to crush me.

"I promise," I whisper, even as a fresh wave of fear coils in the pit of my stomach.

We're still holding each other and a part of me doesn't want Alex to let go. It feels good...too good to be held like this. I want to drink in each heavenly moment of a warm body against mine, the intimacy of human contact.

As Alex pulls away, I find myself missing the warmth of their embrace. It's a poor substitute for the comfort I once found in June's arms - the way his voice would rumble against my ear, laced with a primal need that set my soul ablaze.

The memory of his touch, his kiss, his unwavering devotion, is a phantom limb, aching to be whole once more. I ache to be held by him, to lose myself in the security of his presence, even as I know it's a path that can only lead to ruin.

Yet the ominous note in my hand is a harsh reminder that such luxuries are no longer mine to claim. The demons circle, sensing my vulnerability, their clawed fingers scraping against the fragile walls of my composure.

"He's moved on," they hiss, "cast you aside like the worthless thing you are. Why would he ever want damaged goods like you?"

I grit my teeth, willing the tears not to fall. I can't afford the weakness, the loss of control. Not now, when there are unseen threats lurking in the shadows.

With a deep, steadying breath, I fold the note and tuck it away, out of sight but never out of mind. The demons may taunt, but I refuse to let them break me. I am Cara Briers - artist, sister, survivor. And I will face this new challenge with the same fierce determination that has seen me through every storm.

June may have forsaken me, but I will not let that break what I've rebuilt. Not when there are still battles to be fought, demons to vanquish. I will find a way to protect myself, to uncover the source of these threats, no matter the cost.

For now, I must be strong. I must be vigilant. And perhaps, in time, I will find the courage to open my heart again - to trust, to love, to heal. But that path is mine alone to navigate, free from the shadows that once consumed me.

Chapter 6
June

The soft glow of my phone screen casts an eerie, almost sinister light in the dim room, the only illumination in this self-imposed fortress of solitude. I hunch over the device, my fingers trembling slightly with a mixture of desperation and anticipation as I navigate to the fake social media profile that has become my nightly refuge and torment.

It's a far cry from the polished, refined image of June Deveaux that the world knows - the poised heir to a vast business empire.

But here, in the shadows of my all-consuming obsession, I am stripped bare, reduced to a lovesick fool grasping at the mere digital scraps of a life I can no longer claim as my own.

My breath catches as Cara's latest post fills the screen - a whimsical animation that captures her essence with such piercing clarity it aches to behold. Her humor, her artistry, the way she sees the world - it's all there.

A bittersweet reminder of the woman I fell irrevocably in love with, the woman I've lost.

Yet, even as the animated Cara dances across the screen, I am struck by what is missing. The personal details, the glimpses into her heart that I crave like a drowning man craves air.

The spaces my Cara Mia once occupied, now glaringly empty, taunting me with their blankness.

"Where are you, Cara?" I whisper to the screen, my voice hoarse with desperation. "Who are you sharing your life with now?" The questions hang heavy in the air, unanswered and mocking, stoking the flames of my all-consuming jealousy.

I am a man possessed, driven to the brink of madness by the unknown, by the terrifying possibility that someone else may now be basking in the warmth of Cara's love and affection - a privilege that was once mine, and mine alone.

The thought of her in another's arms is a red-hot poker to my gut, a searing jolt of all-consuming jealousy that threatens to turn my world to ash.

Restless energy coils within me, and I find myself on my feet, pacing the length of my bedroom like a caged predator. The walls seem to close in, suffocating me with their cold, unyielding opulence - a gilded cage that mocks the feverish desperation clawing at my very soul.

Is this how she felt— when she sees pictures of me with Amethyst?

This searing, all-consuming jealousy that leaves nothing but bitter regret in its wake?

I need answers, need them like I need my next breath. And so, I find myself seeking solace in the one place where secrets are currency and information is power - the cigar club, where the elite gather to indulge their basest desires and most twisted obsessions.

The rich, heady scent of leather and tobacco wraps around me like a familiar, seductive embrace as I settle into my usual armchair, my outward appearance a picture of cool composure. But beneath the polished veneer, I am a man on the edge, my nerves thrumming with a desperate, almost feral energy that threatens to consume me whole.

"Jameson, neat," I murmur to the passing waiter, my voice steady even as my hands tremble around the crystal tumbler. The burn of the liquor as it slides down my throat is a welcomed distraction, a momentary reprieve from the clawing need that has become my constant companion.

Across from me, a man with steel-gray hair and a gaze to match regards me with a knowing, almost predatory look. He is a confidant of my father's, a man who trades in secrets and favors, a man who can find out anything for the right price.

"I need your help," I say, cutting straight to the chase, my voice laced with an undercurrent of barely contained anguish. "There's a man, someone close to Cara. I need to know who he is."

The man leans back in his chair, his expression unreadable, but his eyes glint with a spark of dark understanding. "Cara," he repeats, the name rolling off his tongue like a temptation. "The artist, correct? The one you were...seeing?"

I nod, my jaw clenching at the past tense, the implication that what Cara and I shared is now little more than a fleeting memory. "Yes," I say, my voice tight with restrained emotion. "I need to know who she's spending her time with now. It's...personal."

The man regards me for a long, tense moment, his eyes searching mine with an intensity that feels almost invasive. "Personal," he echoes, the word heavy with dark implication. "I see."

He takes a sip of his own drink, the ice clinking softly against the glass. "I'll see what I can find out," he says, his tone measured and professional, yet tinged with a hint of something almost...predatory. "But June...be careful. The road you're walking...it's a dangerous one."

I nod, my heart pounding in my chest, a wild mixture of dread and determination. "I know," I murmur, my voice barely above a whisper. "But I can't...I can't lose her. Not like this."

The man says nothing, but there is a flicker of something akin to sympathy in his eyes - a silent acknowledgment of the depth of my obsession, the lengths I'm willing to go to in order to reclaim what is rightfully mine.

As I leave the club, the weight of my actions settles upon me like a crushing burden, a physical manifestation of the shame and regret that now gnaws at my very soul. The panties, stolen from Cara's laundry line in a moment of unrestrained weakness, burn a hole in my pocket, a constant reminder of how far I have fallen.

The cool night air does little to soothe the fever in my blood as I walk, my mind reeling with the sudden, sickening realization that what had once been a twisted form of love - a desperate need to protect and possess - has morphed into something far darker, something that threatens to consume me whole.

I am no longer the man Cara fell in love with, the man she trusted with her most fragile heart. I am a shadow of myself, a twisted reflection in a funhouse mirror - and the thought of her ever seeing me in this state, the disgust and horror that would surely fill her eyes, is enough to bring me to my knees.

Time slows, each heartbeat thundering in my ears as I stumble, my hand bracing against the rough brick of a nearby building. A wave of nausea rolls through me, leaving me breathless, the reality of my actions, the lines I have crossed, hitting me with the force of a physical blow.

Grief makes good company with the shame that now engulfs me, both emotions sensing my vulnerability, lingering too close for comfort. How could I have let it come to this? How could I have strayed so far from the man I once was, the man I so desperately wanted to be for her?

Tears sting my eyes, blurring the city lights into a hazy kaleidoscope of color, but I blink them away, refusing to grant myself the catharsis of even a single tear. I don't deserve the relief, the absolution - I deserve this pain, this gnawing ache in my chest, a constant reminder of my own failings.

Still, the inky tendril of guilt and shame holds no weight against the all-consuming edict - the promise ingrained into my very soul by these fickle fates sensing my vulnerability. Their orders are loud, their whims wicked, as they conquer the last vestiges of my composure.

The abyss within me yawns wider with each labored step, an endless void that threatens to swallow me whole. Obsession has become my jailer, a relentless taskmaster that cares not for the man I once was, only for the broken shell I've become.

Each breath is a battle, my lungs straining against the weight of my transgressions. I am adrift, a specter haunting the city, a man with no home, no purpose, no future - only this all-consuming fixation that consumes my every waking moment.

The sound of my phone ringing shatters the suffocating silence, jolting me back to reality. I fumble for the device, my heart leaping into my throat as I see Judith's name flashing on the screen.

"Jude," I answer, my voice raw and ragged. "What's up?"

"Oh, you know, just checking in on my baby brother," she says, her tone forcibly light. "Making sure you haven't drowned yourself in a bottle of scotch or something equally dramatic."

I let out a humorless chuckle, running a hand through my hair. "Not yet," I say, the words tasting like ash on my tongue. "But the night is young."

Judith's voice, buoyant and commanding, flows from the speaker, an immediate balm to the chaos that's been my constant companion these days. "Your only sister just got back from vacation. I miss you Junie, get your mopey ass over to the estate."

I grumble into the phone, though the edge of my irritation is already dulling, tempered by the genuine warmth in Judith's laugh.

"It'll be fun, plus I can tell you my game plan," she adds, already knowing I'm never going to pass up an opportunity to see her.

Judith. My sister, my rock, my constant in a world that seems to shift and change with every passing moment. If anyone can understand, can help me find my way back to the light, it's her.

I climb the steps with leaden feet, my heart pounding a frantic rhythm against my ribs. I raise my hand to knock, but before my knuckles can graze the wood, the door swings open, revealing Judith's worried face.

I open my mouth to speak, but the words won't come. They stick in my throat, choking me, drowning me in a sea of my own shame and regret.

But Judith, my beautiful, perceptive sister, seems to understand without me having to say a word. She reaches out, her arms enveloping me in a hug that feels like absolution, like forgiveness, like home.

And there, in the warmth of my sister's embrace, with the weight of my sins pressing down on me like a physical thing, I finally let myself break. The tears come, hot and fast, spilling down my cheeks in a torrent of grief and relief.

I cling to Judith like a drowning man, my face buried in the crook of her neck, my body shaking with the force of my sobs. And she holds me, her hands rubbing soothing circles on my back, her voice a constant murmur of comfort and love.

"I've got you," she whispers, her words a lifeline in the darkness. "I've got you, June. And I'm never letting go."

My body relaxes into the warmth of my sister's anchoring love and I squeeze her tighter.

"Look Drew, I think it's working. He's starting to melt a bit." she teases, leading me into the heart of the house. "Is my warmth not sufficient to thaw that icy heart?"

"You missed your calling as a comedian," I shoot back, but the corners of my mouth betray me, curving into an unwilling smile.

There he is, Drew, lounging like some sort of GQ model reject, drink in hand. He's the picture of relaxed charm, unlike the tension I carry like a second skin.

I accept the drink, if only to have something to do with my hands. "To better navigation and surviving family gatherings," I counter, earning an eye roll from Judith and a puzzled look from Drew.

We settle into an uneasy rhythm, the air filled with Judith's vibrant stories of sun, sand, and the kind of adventures that seem to follow her like devoted puppies. I listen, half-amused, half-envious of her ability to dive headfirst into life's waves while I'm still floundering in the shallows.

Then, as the sun sets, painting the sky with strokes of fire and gold, Judith's tone shifts, the weight of her next words hanging heavily between us.

"I talked to Mom," she begins, her gaze locking with mine, a silent warning of the conversation's gravity. "About you, about... choices."

I stiffen, the familiar surge of defiance rising within me. "And what did the queen decree?"

Judith reaches out, her hand gripping mine, a rare display of vulnerability. "I made a deal with her. I'll marry whoever she wants," she says, her voice steady, but her eyes betraying the cost of her decision. "But only if she lets you be free, June. Free to choose, to love, whoever you want."

The world tilts, the magnitude of her sacrifice rendering me speechless. "Judith, you can't—"

"I can, and I will," she interrupts, her resolve as clear as the Caribbean waters she's just left behind. "Because, Junebug, I want you to be happy, more than anything."

"But, Judith, I..." The words trail off, the enormity of her sacrifice rendering me speechless.

"No buts," she interrupts, her voice softening. "Look, June, I don't know all the ins and outs of what's going on with you and Cara, but I know you. And this," she gestures vaguely, encompassing the estate, our life, "isn't you."

The simplicity of her words, the clarity of her perspective, cuts through the fog that's been suffocating me. In this grand, oppressive home, Judith remains my anchor, the reminder of who I am beneath the Deveaux name.

Drew, who's been silently observing, finally speaks up, his voice grating on my already frayed nerves. "Sounds like a fair deal to me, man. Your sister's taking one for the team."

"You do realize this means she's dumping you, right?" I say, turning to Drew with a pointed look. The words hang in the air, a blend of jest and truth, a test of the levity that has always been our family's unspoken coping mechanism.

Judith's laugh, a genuine burst of amusement, breaks the tension. She gives Drew a sideways glance, one that's both apologetic and teasing. "He's not entirely wrong," she says, the twinkle in her eye betraying her enjoyment of the moment.

Drew, for his part, seems momentarily lost, a deer caught in the Deveaux headlights. But then, realizing the jest, he attempts a chuckle, though it's clear he's out of his depth. "I guess family loyalty really is everything here," he manages, trying to play along.

And for the first time in longer than I can remember, I feel a flickering spark to life in my chest.

A fragile thing, this hope, a smoldering ember in the darkness of my despair. It's a tiny pinprick of light in the overwhelming shadow of my mistakes.

Chapter 7
Cara

It's been weeks since I last saw June since our worlds collided and shattered in that dimly lit restaurant. But the memory of his face, the anguish in his eyes as I walked away, is seared into my mind, a permanent brand on my heart.

And days spent casting furtive glances over my shoulder, jumping at every unexpected sound. Each creak makes my home feel emptier, every distant murmur from the city below, hushed like the blinking of hidden eyes watching my every move.

The evening's shadows lengthen across my small living room, twisting the familiar corners into pools of unease.

I'm curled on the couch, wrapped in a blanket that offers little warmth, but serves as a fragile shield against the growing paranoia seeping into my bones. The TV drones on, a low background hum, but my mind is elsewhere, tracing the ragged edges of my fractured sense of safety.

Wondering if I'm losing my grip on reality... The sudden buzz of my phone breaks the cycle of my anxious thoughts—it's Louis, checking in on me.

"I'm fine, just tired," I type back, the words a half-truth and my phone grows heavy in my hand, yet the only tether to a world I'm no longer certain I belong...or want to be apart of.

A sharp rap at the door jolts my heart into a panicked flight. Then, on learn instinct, I freeze—every muscle coiled tight; ears straining for any hint of danger.

Another insistent knock follows, and I force my feet to carry me to the peephole. The metallic click of the lock sounds thunderous in the charged silence as I turn the knob, with an over exaggerated gulp.

My breath catches in my throat as I pull the door open, only to find no one there - just a small, unassuming package sitting on the threshold.

With trembling hands, I retrieve it, the weight of the parcel belying its innocuous appearance. Tearing open the plain wrapping, I feel my stomach lurch as a single sheet of paper flutters to the floor.

The words, scrawled in a harsh, angular script, seem to leap off the page, a cursive strike intent on wounding, my already battered heart.

"He's not yours anymore. If you know what's good for you, you'll forget Juniper Deveaux ever existed."

My knees buckle, and I sink to the floor, the note clutched in white-knuckled fingers. June's name is a dagger to my soul, a constant, inescapable pain.

A villainous heartache relentlessly consumes; Now a cruel reminder that the past always has a way of clawing its way back—no matter how desperately I try to outrun it.

Rage erupts through me. A living, breathing thing that momentarily overpowers the fear coiled tight in my chest. I push myself upright, the crumpled paper a physical manifestation of my defiance.

How dare they - this faceless, nameless entity - attempt to dictate my life, my heart?

Pacing the length of the room, I feel a sickening dread take root. Is this connected to the strange occurrences - the unexplained glitches, the unsettling sense of being watched, and the missing lingerie that haunts my dreams?

The pieces swirl in my head, a dizzying burst of unanswered questions, when my phone suddenly vibrates again, the familiar name cutting through the haze - Louis, my best friend, the one who has proven himself time and again.

In this moment of turmoil, his call is a lifeline, pulling me out of the web of my own frantic thoughts. Even as my heart aches for June, the man I'll never be good enough to have. So, I cling to every bit of comfort in Louis's steady presence, the reassurance of his unwavering support.

Without hesitation, I answer, the words tumbling out in a rushed torrent. "Lou, I got a note. Someone's threatening me, telling me to stay away from June."

After a tense beat of silence, Louis's voice filters through the speaker, calm and assured. "Okay, Cara, take a deep breath. I'm on my way. We'll figure this out, I promise."

His words ground me in the present even as the specter of June's rejection looms large in my mind.

I nod, even though he can't see me, clinging to the promise of his unwavering support. "Okay," I whisper, the sound of my own voice small and lost.

Sinking back onto the couch, the threatening note still clutched in my trembling hand, I wait.

Each minute that ticks by feels like an eternity, but finally, there's a knock at the door. I pull it open, afraid even as I'm happy to see Louis—his expression etched with concern. As he steps inside, his eyes immediately zero in on the crumpled paper.

"Is that it?" he asks softly, nodding towards the ominous missive.

I nod, handing it to him with a shaky hand. He smooths it out, scanning the words, his jaw clenching with each passing second.

"Cara, this is serious," he says, his voice low and urgent. "We need to call the police. This is harassment, possibly stalking."

I shake my head, sudden panic gripping me. "No, Lou, I can't. I've been too them so many times...they think I'm crazy and there's a padded cell somewhere with name on it."

My voice breaks, and I know too well of the world he comes from...nothing could have prepared me to deal with this.

"You know how these things go. If this is about June, the cesspool deep in the filthy underbelly, his family and lifestyle swims in. The Police will never help, they are basically on payroll." Tears prick at the corners of my eyes, and I will them away refusing to be this weak.

Louis sighs, running a hand through his hair in frustration. "I don't like this, Cara. Someone out there is trying to control you, to isolate you from the people you care about. That's not okay."

"I know," I whisper, my voice cracks again with a tremor of fear. "But I'm scared, Lou. I'm scared of what they might do if I don't listen."

Without hesitation, Louis pulls me into a tight embrace, his strong arms a lifeline in the storm. "I won't let anything happen to you, Cara. I promise. We'll figure this out."

I cling to him, drawing strength from his comfort, allowing his warmth to fortify me against the rising tide of dread.

We stand there for a long moment, two friends offering each other the comfort of shared humanity in the face of an unseen threat. When we finally part, Louis's expression is set and I know that look in his eyes.

"First things first," he says, his tone brooking no argument. "We need to get you somewhere safe. Pack a bag, you're coming to stay with me for a while."

I open my mouth to protest, but he cuts me off with a firm shake of his head.

"Non-negotiable. Until we know exactly what we're dealing with, I'm not letting you out of my sight."

A rush of gratitude—a sensation no combination of words strung together can truly express—chokes me, and I nod.

"Thank you, Lou. I don't know what I'd do without you."

My closest friend offers me a gentle smile, the first genuine one I've seen all night as his eyes light up. "That's what friends are for, Care. Now go pack. I'll make some calls, see if I can dig up anything about where that note came from."

As I hurry to my bedroom, throwing clothes and essentials into a bag, my mind races, struggling to make sense of the twisted turn my life has taken.

Pausing by my dresser, my gaze falls on a framed photo - June and I, caught in a moment of unbridled laughter, our arms wrapped around each other, eyes bright with happiness, and full of mirth that now seems so cruelly out of reach.

I trace a trembling finger over June's face, the cool glass not even close to the heat of June's absent touch and my heart breaks a little more with the fresh reminder of what I want.

Tucking the photo into my bag, I fortify myself using comforting presence of all its sentimental value—the snapshot, a magical talisman against the darkness that threatens to consume me.

I may be running from an unknown stalker, my life upended by fear and uncertainty, but I won't let them take the memories, the love I hold for June. That is mine to keep, no matter what horrors await.

With a deep breath, I shoulder my bag and return to the living room, where Louis waits; his brow furrowed in concentration as he speaks on the phone. Our eyes meet, and he gives me a reassuring nod.

"Ready?" he mouths, his free hand covering the receiver.

I nod, squaring my shoulders. I may be afraid, but I'm not broken. I'm not alone. With Louis by my side, the rock steady foundation of my family and friends' love to bolster me, I can handle all the shit life throws at me.

Even if that means faking a smile, while eating the pain of cutting June out of my soul with reality's rusty blade.

As we step out into the night, the city a glittering expanse before us, I feel a flicker of something akin to safety - a fragile, flickering harness as I freefall in the dark chaos of my life.

But one thing I know, right now... it's enough to keep me putting one foot in front of the other, to nurture the belief that there is a light at the end of this treacherous tunnel.

I may be walking into the unknown, but I'm not making this journey alone.

In the days that follow, Louis takes me under his wing, his home a sanctuary in the storm. The way he knows exactly how much space to give; Or how to distract me from my silent spirals.

I can't help but love how the quiet strength of Louis's reassurance is a beautiful reminder that, I'm not as adrift as I feel.

Yet, even in this newfound safety, the shadows of my past refuse to relinquish their grip. As I sit at Louis's kitchen table, the soft light casting a warm glow over the tidy space, I sense the weight of his unspoken thoughts, the tension that seems to cling to him like a second skin.

I feel like it's my turn to be my friend's anchor, and I can't help but pry. "I kind of heard you arguing earlier. Are you okay?"

Finally, he looks up, his eyes glistening with unshed tears as they meet mine. The usual vibrancy in his gaze is dimmed, replaced by a heaviness that seems to drag him down.

"Cara," he begins, his voice a hoarse whisper laced with the tremor of barely contained emotion, "there's something I need to tell you."

My heart stutters in my chest as I lean in, dread and concern coiling around my ribs like a vice. "What is it, Lou?" I ask softly, reaching out to cover his hand with my own.

He takes a shuddering breath, his fingers tightening almost convulsively around his mug.

For a long, charged moment, the silence stretches between us, pregnant with the weight of his unspoken words. Then, finally, he utters the confession that he probably thinks will irrevocably change the course of our friendship.

"I'm gay."

The words seem to steal the very air from the room, their simple truth crashing down upon me with the force of a tidal wave... But it's not his sexuality, that's the issue.

It's because I see the shame etched into the tense lines of his body, the fear dimming his bright in eyes that have always been windows to Louis' beautiful soul.

Without hesitation, I grasp his hands, holding them firmly between my own. "Hey, look at me," I murmur, waiting until he meets my gaze. "Louis, I love you, no matter what. You're my best friend, and nothing could ever change that."

A single tear slips down his cheek as his face crumples in anguish.

"My family..." he chokes out, each word laced with the pain of rejection. "When I told them, they...they said they never wanted to see me again. That I...disgust them."

The words are a physical blow, stealing the breath from my lungs. This man, this generous and loving soul who has been my anchor through every storm, has faced such cruel abandonment from those who should love him most. White-hot rage and heartbreak war within me, mingling with a profound grief for the pain he has endured.

I slide from my chair, pulling him into the tightest hug I could muster.

"I'm so sorry, Lou," I murmur, my voice thick with emotion. "You didn't deserve that. But you have to know, you'll never be alone again. Me, Sonya, Song...we're your family now. And we love you, all of you, no matter what."

His arms tighten around me, and a sob wrenches free from his trembling form. I hold him close, whispering words of comfort and reassurance, my own tears slipping silently down my cheeks.

Louis is my closest friend, one of the few people I truly trust...and I'll be damned if I let anyone make him feel like anything less than the precious, irreplaceable soul that he is. In that moment, as I cradle him in my arms, I know with unwavering certainty that I will fight tooth and nail to protect him, to shield him from the cruel judgments of this world.

And right there, I make a vow to myself to never let him feel so alone, so unloved again.

The sound of my phone buzzing shatters the heavy silence, and I pull back to see a text from Sonya - a summons to a mandatory family dinner. I can't help the laugh that bubbles up, the tension in the room dissipating like mist in the sun.

"Looks like we've got a family dinner tonight. Mandatory attendance," I tell Louis, showing him the message. His own laughter, bright and genuine, is a balm to my battered psyche.

SAY YOU'LL STAY

I feel lighter than I have in days. Yes, there are still shadows lurking in the corners of my life - an ominous note, a heart torn between past and present - but for the first time in months, I feel truly free.

Free from fear, free from doubt, free from the suffocating grip of an unseen force.

The weight of the past few weeks presses down on me as we stand outside the familiar duplex, the childhood home that has always been my safe haven. And yet, as I cross the threshold, I'm struck by a newfound vulnerability, a sense of being mentally and emotionally compromised that I can't seem to shake.

But I can't let my family see the depths of my struggles - can't let Louis know that his attempts to buoy me have fallen short against the relentless tide of paranoia and dread. So, I step into the warmth of their embrace, the laughter, the chatter, it all fills me with a profound sense of belonging, a reminder that no matter what life throws my way, I have people who care, a safe harbor in the storm.

For a moment, it works - I'm swept up in the comfort of family, my anchors in this turbulent sea. But even as I try to lose myself in the familiar rhythms of home, I can feel the weight of their curious gazes, the unspoken questions lingering in the air.

My family gathers around the dinner table, the conversation flows around me, but I find my thoughts consumed by the events of the past few weeks. The glitches, the notes, the constant, nagging sensation of being followed - they all swirl in my mind, a whirlpool of fear and growing anxiety.

"Earth to Cara," Sonya teases, waving a hand in front of my face. "Where'd you go just now?"

I blink, realizing I've been staring blankly at my plate. "Sorry, I was just...thinking about work," I lie, the words tasting like ashes on my tongue.

But even as I utter the falsehood, I know the truth - my mind is consumed by June, by the aching longing for his steadfast presence, the comfort and security I once found in his embrace.

I can almost picture him here, beside me, his hand on my knee in a silent promise of protection, a rock in the storm. The realization hits me like a sucker punch to the gut, and I feel tears prickling at the corners of my eyes.

Excusing myself, I retreat to the bathroom, letting the dam break as great, shuddering sobs wrack my frame.

I feel like I'm losing my mind, like the very foundations of my world are crumbling beneath me. But even in the depths of my despair, there's a flicker of something else - a fierce, unyielding refusal to let this unseen force break me.

I've come too far, fought too hard, to let someone else dictate the course of my life.

Splashing water on my face, I take a series of deep, steadying breaths, willing my racing heart to calm. When I return to the table, my smile is genuine, if a bit weary. "Sorry about that," I say, my voice stronger than I feel. "I just needed a moment."

Sonya, ever in tune with my shifting moods, reaches out and gives my hand a gentle squeeze under the table. "You know we're here for you, right?" she murmurs, her eyes shining with concern.

I feel a lump form in my throat, overwhelmed by the depth of their love and support. "I know," I manage, offering her a grateful nod.

Song chimes in, his tone gentle but resolute. "Whatever's going on, Cara, you don't have to face it alone. We've got your back, sis."

Their words are a balm to my battered soul, I want to open up, to unburden myself and let them help carry the weight of my fears. But the words stick in my throat, a stubborn reminder that I'm not ready, not yet.

"Thanks, guys," I breathe, my voice thick with emotion. "I know you're here for me. I just...I need a little more time."

They nod, understanding in their eyes.

No demands, no pressure - just an unwavering acceptance that bolsters me, even as I struggle to find the strength to confide in them fully.

As the night wears on, I'm swept up in the familiar ebb and flow of my siblings' playful banter, Louis's quick wit providing a lighthearted counterpoint. The comfortable silences between us is more than welcome.

A needed reminder that I have people who love me, who will be there to catch me when I inevitably fall.

And yet, even amidst the warmth and security of my makeshift family, I can feel the weight of their unspoken questions, the lingering concern in their gazes. They know something is wrong, that I'm shouldering a burden too heavy for one person to bear.

But they also respect my need for space, my right to share my troubles on my own terms.

It's in these quiet moments, when the laughter fades and the conversation lulls, that the ghosts of my past come creeping back - not just June, but the growing sense of unseen eyes tracking my every move.

As I lie in bed that night, I can't help but wonder if I'm truly safe, even here. The missing underwear, swirls in my mind, a disquieting tapestry of beckoning insanity.

The shadows seem to press in, whispering secrets that chill me to the bone. What if the stalker finds me, even in this supposed refuge? What if they make good on their threat, and I lose June forever?

The thought is like a knife to my heart, twisting and tearing.

Despite everything, despite the pain and heartbreak, I still ache for June's presence, the comfort of his strong arms and the reassurance of his unwavering devotion.

Even now, with so much unresolved between us, the mere idea of losing him forever is almost more than I can bear.

Curling into myself, I allow the tears to flow freely, no longer concerned with maintaining a brave face. In the privacy of this room, I let the grief and fear have their way, sobs wracking my body as I mourn the shattered remnants of the life I once knew.

June's face, etched into the photo tucked safely in my bag, is a phantom presence that both haunts and comforts me.

I trace the familiar lines of his features, memorizing every detail, as if committing them to memory could somehow keep him tethered to me, no matter the distance that now lies between us.

"I need you," I whisper into the darkness, my voice small and tremulous. "I still need you, June. Even after everything..."

The admission hangs in the air, a confession that cuts to the quick of my battered heart. I may be surrounded by the love and support of my family, but the truth remains - it is June's presence, his unwavering strength and steadfast devotion, that I crave most in this moment of crisis.

And so, in the quiet solitude of this borrowed room, I allow myself to truly grieve - not just for the threats that now loom over me, but for the shattered remnants of the life I once shared with the man I love.

Tears flow freely, washing away the careful facade I've struggled to maintain, until I'm left raw, exposed, and painfully vulnerable.

But in the midst of this emotional shit storm, an ember of determination begins to smolder, steadily growing brighter with each shuddering breath. I may be afraid, I may be lost, but I refuse to let this unseen force break me.

I am Cara Briers - artist, sister, survivor - and I will face whatever lies ahead with the same fierce resolve that has carried me through every storm.

Tomorrow, I will be strong. Tomorrow, I will fight.

Because now, in the safety of these four walls, I will mourn what I've lost, and steel myself for the battles to come.

Chapter 8
June

The silence of my apartment is oppressive, amplifying the incessant ticking of the antique clock on the mantelpiece. Each second drags like an eternity as I pace restlessly, my phone clutched in a white-knuckled grip, waiting in vain for a reply that never comes.

It's been a week since I last caught a glimpse of Cara through the hidden cameras - her vibrant presence, her intoxicating laugh, all reduced to digital fragments that mock the gaping void in my heart. And now, she's vanished, disappeared without a trace, leaving behind only the ghost of her memory to haunt me.

I've called, I've texted, I've even gone to her apartment, scouring every inch for any sign of her, but it's as if she's been swallowed by the city, leaving me adrift in a sea of unanswered questions. The thought of her out there, in the arms of another man, twists like a knife in my gut, jealousy and regret warring within me in a vicious, unrelenting dance.

Is she safe? Does she think of me, even for a moment, as I do of her, every waking breath? Or has she found solace, the comfort and security I so desperately long to provide, in the embrace of the one who lured her away? The image of her with that man flashes through my mind, a searing brand of jealousy that sets my blood to boiling.

I should have fought for her, should have proven my love, my devotion, beyond any shadow of a doubt. But instead, I let her slip through my fingers, watch her walk away, my own failings tearing us apart. A guttural growl escapes my lips, my fist clenching as volcanic wrath courses through my veins.

"A little too late for that now, buddy," I mutter, the words laced with bitter irony as I sink back onto the couch, the anger fading with each syllable. My head falls into my hands, tremors wracking my frame as the weight of my mistakes presses down upon me like an oppressive physical force.

How could I have been so blind, so foolishly, selfishly complacent? I'd taken Cara for granted, assumed she would always be there, waiting in the wings of my life, ready to receive the scraps of affection I deigned to offer. But now, faced with the harsh reality of her absence, I'm painfully, viscerally aware of just how integral she is to the very fabric of my being.

A sudden knock at the door jolts me from my spiraling thoughts, and my heart pounds with a desperate, almost feverish hope.

Could it be her, returned to me at last? I wrench open the door, Cara's name trembling on my lips - but it's not the woman I ache for who stands before me.

Instead, it's Judith, my sister, her features etched with a concern that mirrors the turmoil raging within me. "June," she says, stepping inside and closing the door behind her. "We need to talk."

I nod, my throat constricted, and lead her to the living room. She perches on the edge of the armchair, her piercing gaze searching mine, as if trying to divine the depths of my inner turmoil.

"You have to come back to the company," she says softly, her voice laced with an understanding that only makes the ache in my chest more profound. "I know things are tough for you right now. But I need you..."

A strangled sound escapes my lips, a fractured blend of laughter and sobs. "I don't know what to do, Jude," I confess, the admission tearing at my pride. "I don't know how to be the man I need to be, not when I have to find a way to make this right with Cara."

Judith leans forward, her hand covering mine in a gesture of comfort and support. "June, I know you're hurting," she murmurs, "but you have to think about this from my perspective. And Cara...she's been through so much. She needs time to heal, to find herself again, without the weight of our family's baggage."

I nod, the bitter truth of her words a pill I can scarcely swallow. "I know, Jude. But I...I've made mistakes, done things I'm too ashamed to even confess to you. And yet, I love her, more than I ever imagined possible. I can't lose her, not like this."

Judith sighs, her eyes softening with empathy. "I know, June. But sometimes, loving someone means letting them go, giving them the space to find their own way back to you. If what you have is truly meant to be, she'll come back to you when she's ready."

I close my eyes, feeling the hot sting of tears as they spill down my cheeks. "And what if she doesn't?" I whisper, the fear of that possibility a lead weight in the pit of my stomach. "What if I've lost her for good?"

Judith gives my hand a reassuring squeeze, an anchor in the tempestuous sea of my emotions. "Then you'll find a way to move forward, to become the man she always knew you could be. You'll learn from this, grow from it, and maybe, just maybe, you'll find each other again someday."

I let her words wash over me, a fragile glimmer of hope amidst the overwhelming despair. She's right, as much as the admission pains me - I can't force Cara to return to me, can't make her love me again. That decision lies solely in her hands, and all I can do is strive to be worthy of her trust, her affection, when the time comes.

"What better way to distract yourself than with busy boardrooms and exciting acquisitions?" Judith says, a faint trace of jest in her tone, though I can sense the desperation underlying her words.

Judith would never try to manipulate me, not like this - there must be something truly dire that requires both Deveaux heirs at the helm of the family business.

As I take my place in the gilded office, the expansive windows offering a panoramic view of the city below, I'm struck by the stark contrast between the opulence that surrounds me and the chill that now seeps through my veins. The leather of the oversized chair, once a symbol of power and success, now feels like a stifling, unyielding prison.

My fingers drum an erratic rhythm on the polished oak of the desk, a jarring counterpoint to the steady, confident tempo that would have graced my father's hands. Each beat is a harsh reminder - I'm merely a substitute in this game, a player tasked with navigating a labyrinth of unforgiving rules and monumental stakes that I never asked to inherit.

I sift through the documents cluttering the desk, each one a serpent coiled in paper form, hissing accusations of negligence and financial ruin. My father's words, once a guiding light, now echo like distant, ominous thunder - a storm I can scarcely hope to outrun. "Lead with integrity, June. Remember, you're a Deveaux." But what does that mean when the very foundation of the empire he built stands upon a crumbling edifice of lies and deception?

I pause, a report catching my eye - numbers that refuse to add up, no matter how many times I review them. My stomach twists with a visceral response to the inevitable fallout that awaits, the air in the room feeling thinner, as if the glass walls are closing in, trapping me in a suffocating aquarium where I'm both predator and prey.

But it's exhausting, this charade - every fake smile, every staged photograph, a piece of my authentic self slipping away, sacrificed upon the altar of public perception and familial duty.

The silence remains, a mocking companion to my solitary confinement at the pinnacle of this towering edifice.

I allow myself a moment of weakness, leaning back in the chair, my head in my hands as the weight of the Deveaux legacy presses down upon me with a relentless, crushing force.

In this gilded cage, I find myself envying Cara - her freedom, her escape from the shackles that now bind me. A bitter laugh escapes my lips, the sound hollow and foreign. Love, freedom, choice - such luxuries are the domain of those unburdened by the thorned crowns and golden fetters that define my existence.

I rise, a mechanical motion, and catch sight of my reflection in the glass - a stranger cloaked in bespoke suits and unearned authority.

The city below, with its twinkling lights and shadowed streets, feels a world away, a mosaic of lives untouched by the tempest that rages within my ivory tower.

But it's in this moment of profound isolation, with the night encroaching upon the empire of glass and steel, that a spark of defiance ignites within me. I am June Deveaux, yes, but I will be so on my own terms, not as a mere pawn in this game of dynasties and deception.

With a renewed sense of direction, I turn to face the night skyline, the city no longer a witness to my faltering, but a challenge to be met. The road ahead is fraught with battles, both internal and external, but I'm done being a mere pawn in a game of dynasties and deception.

"I will find a way," I whisper to the city, to myself. "For you, Dad. For me."

Restlessness is my constant companion as I pace the confines of my office, the stormy thoughts churning in my mind an incessant undercurrent that refuses to be silenced. In the privacy of this space, under the cloak of night, I battle with the memories, the remnants of a past that cling to me like a stubborn veil.

In my pocket, Cara's panties - a fragment I'm both desperate to hold onto, and terrified to acknowledge - serve as a visceral reminder of the complexity that now defines my existence.

It's just a skimpy scrap of fabric, yet it represents so much more: the memories we've made, the desires we've shared, the regrets that now haunt me.

The scent of Cara that had once clung to the delicate lace has long since been replaced by the bitter, isolating reality of my current circumstances.

It's a cruel, taunting reminder that the world I once knew, the life I shared with the woman I love, has been irreversibly altered.

I'm a man divided, torn between the gnawing need to move forward and the inescapable pull of the past. Cara's image haunts me, an indelible mark seared into the very fabric of my being.

I miss her, more than I've ever allowed myself to admit - the sound of her laughter, the warmth of her touch, the radiant light that shone in her eyes.

All snapshots of a time that now seems both impossibly distant and hauntingly close.

My laptop sits upon the desk, an unassuming portal to a multitude of responsibilities and, paradoxically, a means of escape. I hesitate, caught in the grip of an internal turmoil that finds me grappling with the ethics of my intended course of action.

I'm not here for company secrets or business strategies; no, my purpose is far more selfish, far more desperate. I seek a balm for the ache that has settled deep within my soul - a cure for the longing that threatens to consume me whole.

The blurred line between concern and invasion has left me navigating a murky moral landscape I never intended to enter.

A part of me recoils at the very idea, screaming for me to stop, to turn away. This isn't the man I want to be - skulking in shadows, clinging to a past that, by all rights, should remain just that.

The thought of betraying Cara's trust, of infringing upon her privacy in such a fundamental way, should be a wake-up call, a glaring red flag warning me away from this path. And yet, desperation has a way of eroding even the strongest of my resolve.

I rationalize the action, convincing myself that it's mere concern, a check-in to ensure her safety, nothing more.

My fingers hover over the keyboard, trembling slightly, before giving in to the compulsion that drives me. The screen flickers to life, revealing the scenes of a life that had once been so intimately intertwined with my own.

There she is - Cara, her vibrant presence a balm to the fire that rages within me, even through the grainy lens of the hidden cameras. I tell myself it's concern, that the tightening in my chest is fear for her well-being, and not the desperate echo of a longing I've tried in vain to extinguish.

She's blissfully unaware of the eyes upon her, living in a bubble of privacy that I've shattered with my own selfish actions. Guilt gnaws at the edges of my consciousness, but it's drowned out by the louder, more insistent voice of desperation, of aching need. I watch, telling myself that this will be the last time, even as I've uttered that same lie to myself time and time again.

My fingers fumble with the belt, the clinking sound echoing in the silence of the office like a prelude to the symphony of pleasure that awaits. As I unfasten my pants, freeing my aching cock from its confines, a shiver of anticipation runs down my spine, stoking the base instincts that now threaten to consume me.

I wrap my hand around the throbbing length, savoring every inch as if it were Cara's own soft touch surrounding me.

A slow stroke starts at the base, trailing up along the thick vein that pulsates with each heartbeat until reaching the swollen tip slick with pre-cum. With agonizing slowness, I begin to stroke, each pump of my fist a mimicry of the delicate movements I remember from our past trysts.

"Fuck," I groan, the sound low and guttural, as I caress the sensitive flesh, imagining the way Cara's lips would part, her tongue flickering teasingly over the swollen head. My palm glides over the slick, throbbing skin, heightening the pleasurable friction until I'm drunk on the sensations.

Images of Cara flood my mind - the lush curve of her lips, the intoxicating depth of her gaze as she looks up at me, her hands holding me steady. The very thought sends waves of lust crashing through me, a begging demand to be sated.

Growling low in my throat, I picture her lithe body stretched out beneath mine, arching into each thrust as I plunge into her welcoming heat.

"So tight... so damn sweet," I grunt, my pace quickening to match the phantom rhythm of our shared fantasies.

My other hand travels south, cupping and massaging; The slide of her panties on my heavy balls, adds another layer of sensation that brings me ever closer to the edge.

It's as if I can feel Cara's deft fingers there, driving me mad with their expert touch.

A harsh gasp escapes my lips as I envision her on all fours, muscles straining with each punishing thrust. The memory of her sinful moans, the way they would seep into my very being and ignite a fire within me, echoes in my ears, spurring me on.

"Harder... take it harder," I growl, the words a commanding refrain as my pace quickens, the grip on my cock tightening. And then, as if I can feel the quiver of her body around mine, the tension within me reaches a crescendo.

Pleasure crashes over me in a tidal wave, my release spilling forth in hot, thick spurts that coat my stomach. I'm left panting, reeling from the intensity of my climax, but even as the afterglow begins to fade, I can't help but feel a twinge of regret.

Will this ever be enough? Will I ever have more than these fleeting, secretive rendezvous to sustain the inferno of my desire for Cara?

The thought leaves a bitter taste in my mouth as I set about cleaning the evidence of my indulgence.

With each wipe, I'm confronted by the gnawing emptiness that lingers within me, a void that no amount of self-gratification can ever hope to fill. Until I can make this fantasy a reality once more, these nightly rituals will have to suffice - a bittersweet sanctuary for the love I hold for my sweet Cara Mia.

Time seems to blur together in an endless cycle of meetings, paperwork, and calculated public appearances; The weight of my father's failing health hangs over me like a dark cloud.

The cloying scent of Amethyst's perfume assaults my senses the moment she glides into the office, a calculated intrusion that sets my nerves on edge. I grit my teeth, willing myself to maintain the practiced veneer of composure as her manicured fingers graze my arm in a gesture meant to soothe, but only serves to ignite the smoldering embers of my irritation.

"How are you holding up, June?" she purrs, her voice dripping with a feigned concern that fails to reach the calculating glint in her eyes.

"Could you not be so...you right now?" I snap, the words laced with thinly veiled disdain. "Sit down, look pretty - that's what my mom pays you for, isn't it?"

Amethyst's brow furrows slightly, a flicker of hurt flashing across her features before she smooths her expression into a practiced mask of concern. "June, I'm only trying to help. You seem—"

"Help?" I interrupt, my voice sharp and mirthless. "The only way you can help is by leaving me the hell alone for once." I gesture sharply toward the chair across from me. "Just be a good little ornament; because if you leave now, Elaine will appear. So sit the fuck down and shut up Amethyst. That's all I need from you right now."

She hesitates, seemingly taken aback by my uncharacteristic curtness, but ultimately complies, settling into the chair with a measured grace that only serves to further grate on my nerves. The silence that stretches between us is pregnant with tension, a charged stillness that I refuse to be the first to break.

Amethyst's gaze remains trained on me, unwavering, and I can feel the weight of her scrutiny like a physical force, pressing down upon me until I'm fighting the overwhelming urge to squirm under its intensity. The air in the room feels thick, stifling, as if the very walls are closing in, trapping me in this parade of expectation and obligation.

I force myself to hold her gaze, to project an air of calm that I'm far from feeling. But beneath the surface, my emotions are a raging tempest - frustration, resentment, and a deep, gnawing longing for the freedom and authenticity I once knew in Cara's embrace.

Chapter 9
Cara

My heart is heavy with worry and an overwhelming sense of déjà vu as I navigate the sterile hallways of the hospital. The last time I found myself in a place like this, I was visiting my own father, a memory that still stings with the raw, unhealed wound of loss.

But today, it's not my family that brings me to this sterile purgatory of sickness and sorrow. It's June's.

The news of his father's sudden hospitalization spread through the city like wildfire, and before I could even pause to second-guess my actions, I found my feet carrying me here, to this moment, to him.

I spot June at the end of the hallway, his proud shoulders uncharacteristically slumped under the weight of his father's condition. He's not alone. Judith, his ever-present sister, stands beside him, her hand resting on his arm in a gesture of comfort and support that sends a pang of jealousy through my heart.

Approaching slowly, I'm suddenly unsure of my place in this tableau of familial grief. "June," I say softly, my voice barely above a whisper, as if speaking too loudly might shatter the fragile moment.

He turns, those striking eyes that once held such warmth and love now guarded and shuttered. For a fleeting instant, as our gazes lock, I'm transported back to a time when those emerald depths sparkled with laughter and promised forever. But now, they reflect only the harsh glare of the hospital lights and a wall of stoic distance.

The silence stretches between us, heavy with unspoken words and shattered dreams. I search his face for a clue, a sign of the June I once knew so intimately, but I'm met with an impenetrable facade of cold composure.

Judith's voice cuts through the suffocating tension like a scalpel. "Cara, now is not the best time." Her words, though not unkind, are firm, a clear boundary being drawn, a line in the sand separating me from their world of wealth and privilege.

I nod, swallowing past the lump of emotions lodged in my throat. "I understand. I just wanted to..." My voice trails off, any words I might offer feeling wholly inadequate in the face of their pain.

An awkward silence descends, the beeping of monitors and distant chatter of hospital staff a jarring contrast to the loaded stillness between us. And then, as if summoned by the very discomfort that hangs in the air, Amethyst appears, her designer heels clicking on the linoleum floor like a mocking metronome, marking the rhythm of my own mounting unease.

"June, darling," she purrs, placing a perfectly manicured hand on his chest in a gesture that's both possessive and comforting, a silent declaration of her place in his life. Those cold, calculating eyes shift to me, appraising, assessing, a predator sizing up a potential threat. "Cara, what a surprise to see you here."

I feel the heat of humiliation creeping up my neck, the implication of my presence, of the history I share with June, hanging heavy in the charged air. "I just wanted to offer my support," I manage, the words sounding flimsy and insufficient even to my own ears.

Amethyst's smile is tight, a mere formality stretched across her flawless features. "How kind of you." The words are polite, but the underlying tension crackles like electricity, a silent warning to keep my distance.

I turn back to June, desperation clawing at my heart, searching for a sign of the connection we once shared, a flicker of the love that consumed us both. But he remains silent, his gaze now fixed on a point over my shoulder, a clear and cutting dismissal.

The hospital walls seem to close in around me, the air growing thin and suffocating. "I should go," I mumble, the words bitter on my tongue, a surrender I never wanted to make. "I'm sorry for intruding."

As I walk away, each step echoing the growing chasm between us, I feel the weight of our shattered history bearing down on me. The tears I've been holding back threaten to fall, but I blink them away furiously, refusing to let them be a spectacle in this place of sorrow and loss.

The dismissal lands like a physical blow, stealing the breath from my lungs and any last, desperate hope of reconciliation. It's a scene I've played out in my mind countless times, a painful déjà vu of our last encounter, but the reality is so much more visceral, more soul-crushing.

With every step, I feel the distance between us growing, an uncrossable expanse filled with broken promises and unspoken goodbyes. The June I knew, the man who held my heart in his hands, now feels like a distant memory, a beautiful mirage that dissipates in the harsh light of reality.

Tears burn behind my eyes, blurring my vision, but I refuse to let them fall. Not here, not now. I've already shed too many tears for a man who seems content to let our love fade into the shadows of his gilded new life.

Bursting out of the hospital doors, I'm greeted by the chaotic pulse of the city, oblivious to the shattered remnants of my heart scattered on the unforgiving pavement. I hail a cab, seeking solace in the anonymity of the backseat, desperate to escape the suffocating weight of my own emotions.

I close my eyes, exhaling a shaky breath as I try to compose the fractured pieces of my heart.

This is not the ending I envisioned for us, not the future I clung to in the secret corners of my heart. But perhaps it's the inevitable conclusion to our story, a tale of almost and could-have-beens, of two souls who orbited each other but could never quite align.

Even as I try to convince myself to let go, to sever the ties that bind me to him, I know that a part of me will always belong to June. He's etched into my very essence, a permanent scar on my heart, a reminder of the love we shared and the dreams we dared to build.

So I carry on, a woman torn between two worlds, one foot anchored in the present while the other remains forever tethered to a past I cannot forget, no matter how hard I try to bury it beneath the weight of my new reality.

The memories rise unbidden, flickering through my mind like the reel of an old film. Stolen moments of passion, whispered promises in the dark, the searing heat of June's touch branding my skin, marking me as his own. I can still feel the ghost of his lips on mine, the way his strong hands gripped my hips as he drove into me with a fevered urgency, consuming me, claiming me, body and soul.

The ache between my thighs is a cruel reminder of what I've lost, a phantom pain that throbs in time with the shattered beats of my heart. I cross my legs, pressing my thighs together in a futile attempt to ease the throbbing need, but it only serves to intensify the bittersweet ache of longing.

I know I should let him go, shed the memories of our love like a snake shedding its skin, but I cling to them still, a masochistic reminder of the happiness I once held in my grasp. June Deveaux is a drug I cannot quit, an addiction that courses through my veins, leaving me desperate and wanting.

The cab ride stretches on, the city blurring past in a haze of neon and concrete, but I'm lost in a world of my own making, trapped in the labyrinth of my memories and the ruins of my shattered heart. I don't know how to extricate myself from the hold he has on me, how to unravel the tangled threads of our history and emerge whole on the other side.

All I know is that I love him still, with a fierce and desperate intensity that consumes me, even as it tears me apart. And somewhere deep down, in a secret, hidden place I barely dare to acknowledge, a flicker of hope still burns, a stubborn ember that refuses to be extinguished.

Maybe, just maybe, our story isn't over yet. Maybe there's still a chance for redemption, for forgiveness, for a love that can rise from the ashes of our shared past. But for now, I am left to navigate this new reality alone, to piece together the shattered remnants of my heart and learn to breathe again in a world without June by my side.

The cab pulls up to my building, and I step out onto the familiar sidewalk, feeling like a stranger in my own life. The journey upstairs to my apartment is a blur, my feet moving on autopilot as my mind remains mired in the events of the day.

As I close the door behind me, the silence of my empty home crashes over me like a suffocating wave. I lean back against the solid wood, finally allowing the tears to flow freely, hot rivulets of grief and anger and longing cascading down my cheeks.

I sink to the floor, my legs no longer able to support the weight of my anguish, and I let the sobs wrack my body, a primal release of all the pent-up emotions I've been holding inside. The pain is a living, breathing thing, clawing at my insides, tearing me apart with ruthless efficiency.

I don't know how long I stay there, curled up on the cold, hard floor, lost in the maelstrom of my own misery. Minutes, hours, an eternity - time loses all meaning in the face of such devastating heartbreak.

But eventually, the tears subside, leaving me hollow and spent, an empty shell of the woman I once was. I drag myself up, stumbling to the bedroom on unsteady legs, and collapse onto the bed that still holds the faint scent of June's cologne.

I burrow into the sheets, clutching his pillow to my chest like a lifeline, and let the exhaustion of my grief pull me under, into a restless, dreamless sleep. Tomorrow will come, as it always does, and I will have to face this new reality, this life without June by my side.

But for now, in the quiet stillness of my bedroom, I allow myself this moment of weakness, this brief respite from the pain that threatens to consume me whole. For now, I will cling to the memories of our love, to the bittersweet echoes of a passion that burned too bright to last.

The days tick by with a leaden weight, each one a battle against the ever-present gloom that clings to my every step. Yet, amidst the darkness, there are rare glimmers - sparks of joy that remind me I'm more than just the shattered remnants of my broken dreams.

My phone erupts in a frenzy of notifications, an endless cascade of likes and comments. Somebody's shared one of my latest pieces, and it's gone *viral*.

Hands trembling, I scroll through the outpouring, drinking in the words of praise from strangers whose can relate to all the fucked up humor, and release of emotions I've poured into my art.

A bittersweet victory, this unexpected success. Validation of my talents, yes, but a complete different to the personal turmoil still threatening to drown me.

Part of me longs to share this triumph with Mom or Louis, those pillars of unwavering support. But the mere *thought* of opening up, baring my inner demons...no, I couldn't.

"I can already hear Sonya's squeals of joy," I mutter to myself, a wry smile tugging at the corner of my mouth. But the brief flicker of levity is quickly extinguished by the harsh reality. How can I possibly explain the shadows that haunt me, the lingering unease that refuses to let go?

Just last night, as I stumbled half-asleep to the bathroom, I *swear* I saw a figure retreat from the edge of my bed, vanishing into the inky darkness like a specter. The phantom touch of that unwanted presence still lingers on my skin, a shiver of revulsion coursing through me.

Confusion and fear battle within, leaving me unmoored, unbalanced in the one place I should feel safest. I *want* to confide in my loved ones, seek their comfort and reassurance. But stubborn pride, my armor against June's rejection, holds me back. I can't appear *weak*, *broken* in their eyes - not when I've fought so hard to keep my head above water.

So I trudge onward, burying myself in my work - a tenuous lifeline, a fragile raft adrift in the stormy seas of my personal turmoil. It's *mine*, a sanctuary where I can momentarily escape the shadows that haunt my every step. The scratch of pencil against paper, the soft whisper of paint on canvas - these are the sounds that drown out the chaos, if only for a little while.

The accolades keep pouring in, a stream of validation that *should* fill me with pride and a sense of accomplishment. Yet, as I read through the comments, I can't help but wonder - *what would June think?* Would he be pleased, *proud*, of the success I've found, or would it only serve as a painful reminder of the distance that now yawns between us?

The *ache* of missing him is a constant, a phantom limb I can't seem to excise from the very fabric of my being. I *miss* him, *ache* for him, with a ferocity that leaves me breathless. And in the quiet moments, when the din of the city fades and my defenses are lowered, I find myself reaching for the phone, fingers poised to dial his number, to plead for his forgiveness, his *return*.

But reason and pride always win out, snatching the device from my grasp before I can make that fateful call. I can't - *won't* - be the one to initiate contact, not when the memory of his cold dismissal still burns like acid in my veins. If June wants me back, if he still harbors even a glimmer of the love we once shared, then *he* must be the one to bridge the chasm that now separates us.

The shadows linger, a menacing presence that sets my nerves on edge with every passing day. I find myself jumping at sudden noises, my gaze constantly sweeping the room, searching for any sign of the unwanted watcher that seems to dog my every move.

"Get a grip, Cara," I chide myself, running a hand through my tangled hair in frustration. "It's just your imagination running wild. There's no one there."

But the words ring hollow, even to my own ears. It's *maddening* , this growing paranoia, this all-consuming fear that someone - *something* - is out there, watching, *waiting*. I long to confide in Louis, to seek his steadfast support and counsel, but the stubborn pride that has become my armor refuses to let me appear weak, *vulnerable* in his eyes.

And so, I soldier on, a fragile façade of strength masking the turmoil that threatens to consume me from within. The viral acclaim for my work brings me no true joy, only a hollow echo of accomplishment that is quickly drowned out by the ever-present specter of my personal demons.

June's absence is a gaping wound, a void that no amount of professional success can ever hope to fill. I find myself aching for his presence, his steady support, the way his mere existence seemed to ground me, to anchor me in a world that has become increasingly unsteady, *untrustworthy*.

"Ugh, get it together, Cara," I groan, flopping back onto the bed and burying my face in his pillow, still faintly scented with the lingering traces of *him*. "He's gone, and he's not coming back. Time to move the fuck on."

But the words ring hollow, a desperate attempt to convince myself of a truth I'm not ready to accept. June is *gone* , lost to me, a victim of my own stubborn pride and the cruel machinations of fate.

Chapter 10
June

Desperation clings to me like a second skin as I melt into the shadows, my eyes boring into the entrance of Cara's tiny home. Every fiber of my being is consumed by an all-encompassing need to see her.

To be near her - even as the rational part of my mind screams that this is wrong, that I'm crossing lines I can never return from.

But in the twisted maze of my mind, where grief and obsession intertwine, rationality has no place, lost in the labyrinth...trapped in limbo. The doctors' words replay on a loop, a mocking refrain: "A few days, at most." My father, the indomitable Magnus Deveaux, reduced to a ticking clock, his life measured in fleeting hours.

And so I cling to this obsession, this sickening surveillance, as if Cara's presence, even stolen through a lens, can somehow fill the yawning chasm that my father's impending death has carved into my soul.

When she finally emerges, my heart seizes in my chest. But she's not alone. That man— the sight of this nameless thief, walks beside her, their bodies moving in a way that speaks of intimacy, of a bond that I can scarcely bear to acknowledge.

It's in the way both bodies orbit each other with a casual intimacy that rakes across my raw nerves like shards of glass. Their laughter cuts through me like a jagged blade, a parody of the music Cara and I once made together, rips through me, shredding me from the inside out.

Staggering back, I choke on the bitter tang of bile and impotent rage threatening to drag me under.

Somehow, I make it to my car, gripping the steering wheel until my knuckles turn white, as if this small act of physical control could stabilize the world crumbling beneath my feet.

The journey back to the office is a blur of neon smears and blaring horns, the cacophony of the city drowned out by the tempest raging in my skull. Thoughts of my father's imminent demise, the empire's decay, and the sickening certainty that I've lost the only light in my darkness all bleed together, a noose of despair tightening around my throat with each labored breath.

I practically fall into my office chair, a marionette with tangled strings, as the walls close in, the very air thick with the weight of my failures.

But amidst the maelstrom of misery, one truth emerges with crystal clarity: Cara is mine, now and forever, and I will move heaven and hell to bind her to me, to make her see that our fates are irrevocably entwined.

The silence presses in, a physical weight mirroring the suffocating anguish in my chest. And yet, even in this hell, a single thought crystallizes with terrifying clarity: I will not lose Cara.

I will bind her to me, by any means necessary, until she understands that we are inevitable, that our souls are entwined beyond the petty constraints of morality or reason.

Days bleed into weeks as I dedicate myself to this twisted ritual, a slave to the compulsions that have consumed me. The hidden cameras in Cara's apartment spring to life, a voyeuristic window into the life

I'm determined to reclaim as my own; a paltry slave to the addiction I have to my Cara Mia.

She *belongs* with me, *needs* me, even if she doesn't realize it yet.

As my father's condition deteriorates, I find myself splitting my time between the cold, sterile halls of our family home and the equally cold glow of my computer screen. The once vibrant rooms now echo with the whispers of death, a makeshift hospice for my father's final days.

I sit by his bedside, watching the rise and fall of his chest, each breath a Herculean effort. My mother and Judith flit in and out, their faces etched with sorrow and exhaustion.

But I remain, a silent sentinel, my hand clasped around my father's, as if my touch alone could anchor him to this world. It's during one of these vigils, as the shadows lengthen and the machines hum their morbid lullaby, that my father takes his last, shuddering breath.

The great Magnus Deveaux, a titan of industry and pillar of strength, slips away into the void; leaving us all in a sea of grief without a sail, or compass.

Tears burn hot trails down my cheeks, blurring the faces of my mother and sister into indistinct smears of sorrow.

I don't know how long I sit there, cradling my father's lifeless hand, before the world fades away, the edges of my vision darkening until there's nothing but an all-consuming void.

When I come back to myself, I'm standing in Cara's apartment. My heart pounds against my ribs, a frantic drumbeat that echoes in my ears, as the familiar scent of her envelops me - vanilla and cinnamon, with a hint of something uniquely Cara that I can never quite define.

I move through her space like a wraith, my footsteps muffled by the plush carpet. Every inch of this place is seared into my memory, a tapestry woven from stolen moments and secret longings. How many hours have I spent watching her through the unblinking eye of the camera, a silent sentinel in the shadows?

But tonight, watching is no longer enough. The ache in my chest, the yawning void left by my father's passing, demands more. It demands her presence, her touch, her love - even if I have to steal it like a thief in the night.

I find her in the bedroom, a vision of beauty amidst the chaos that rages in my soul. For a moment, I simply stand there, drinking her in, my eyes devouring every curve and hollow of her petite frame.

At 5'0", she's always been the perfect size for me to sweep off her feet, to tuck under my chin and shield from the world. This delicate, ethereal creature whose mere existence has the power to both soothe and scorch my soul.

Cara, my muse, my *everything* - reduced to flesh and blood, a living embodiment of the dreams that have both sustained and tormented me.

I can practically taste the sweetness of her skin on my tongue, the velvet caress of her raven hair against my cheek. *Mine*, the word pulses through me like a primal drumbeat, a claim I will fight to the death to defend.

"I'm here. You hear me?" I breathe, my voice hardly more than a whisper. "I'll always be here. You're mine, do you understand? Mine."

With trembling fingers, I reach out to trace the line of her cheek, marveling at the silky smoothness of her skin. She stirs slightly at my touch, a breathy sigh escaping her lips, and I freeze, my heart lodged in my throat.

But she doesn't wake, lost in the depths of her dreams, and I release a shuddering breath.

Slowly, carefully, I ease myself onto the bed beside her, the mattress dipping under my weight. This close, the heat of her body is like a furnace, searing me to my very core. I can feel the whisper of her breath against my cheek, the steady rise and fall of her chest, and it's almost more than I can bear.

"My Cara Mia," I murmur, my voice hoarse with longing. "If you only knew how every beat of my heart is a cry for your touch, your love."

The words pour out of me like a prayer, a confession of all the dark and desperate things I've kept locked inside for so long. In the shadows of this room, with only the moon as my witness, I lay myself bare, stripped of all pretense and guile.

"I'm lost without you," I whisper, my lips a hairsbreadth from her ear. "You're the only hope I have left., the only light I see. Please, Cara. Please come back to me."

A single tear slips down my cheek, hot and scalding. It falls on her skin, a glistening trail of my sorrow, my desperation. I long to gather her in my arms, to crush her to my chest and never let go.

But even in the depths of my madness, I know that I cannot, will not cross that final, irreversible line.

Instead, I content myself with this stolen moment, this illicit communion. I memorize the curve of her cheek, the fan of her lashes, the delicate tracery of veins beneath her translucent skin. I breathe her in, letting her scent fill my lungs, my very soul.

Time loses all meaning as I lie there, drowning in her presence. The world outside this room, with all its pain and chaos, fades away until there is only her, only us, suspended in a cocoon of shadows and silence.

But even as I try to lose myself in the fantasy, reality intrudes, cold and unforgiving. Cara stirs, a soft moan escaping her lips, and panic seizes me in an icy grip.

I can't let her find me here, can't bear to see the shock and revulsion in her eyes when she realizes the depths to which I've sunk. With a silent curse, I force myself to pull away, to disentangle my body from the warmth of hers.

Every fiber of my being screams in protest as I slip from the bed, my skin aching from the loss of her touch. I stand over her, my chest heaving, drinking in one last, desperate glimpse of her sleeping form.

"I love you," I breathe, the words a vow and a prayer. "I will always love you, no matter what. And I swear, on my father's grave, that I will find a way to be the man you deserve. The man you once believed me to be."

With those words, I force myself to turn away, to slip out of her room as silently as I came. The cool night air is a shock to my system as I step outside, a brutal reminder of the reality I've been trying so hard to escape.

I will have to claw my way out of the abyss of my own making. But for her, for the chance to hold her in my arms and know that I am worthy of her love, there is no price too high, no sacrifice too great.

Cara, my heart, my home - I'm coming back to you. Not as the broken, twisted wretch I am now, but as the man you once saw in me, the man I swear I will become once more.

For you, my love, I will move mountains. I will reshape the very fabric of my being, even in the depths of my own personal hell; because I know: This isn't over, Cara. You *belong* with me. *Soon, my love.*

Soon, you will be mine again.

The days that follow my violation of Cara's sanctuary pass in a haze of guilt, grief, and an all-consuming desperation that threatens to drown me. I find myself torn, caught in a maelstrom of conflicting impulses - the rational part of my mind screaming for me to seek help.

To make amends, while the twisted, grief-stricken edges of my psyche cling to the deluded fantasy that Cara is destined to be *mine*, no matter the cost.

I bury myself in work, burying the sickening reality of my actions beneath the towering stacks of paperwork and frenzied meetings that now consume my waking hours.

The opulent halls of the Deveaux empire, close in around me as I struggle to keep up the façade of calm competence. But the cracks in my composure are ever-widening, visible in the tremor of my hands, the haunted shadows that linger in my gaze.

Yet, I cannot - *will not* - risk exposing the depths of my depravity, the twisted, all-consuming fixation on Cara that has become the very beating of my corrupted heart.

The mere thought of their disappointment, their *disgust*, is enough to send me reeling, reinforcing the walls I've so meticulously constructed around the festering rot at my core.

And so, I press on, a specter in my own life, going through the motions of a man in control even as I feel the very ground crumbling beneath my feet. Amethyst attempts to breach the fortress of my isolation, her delicate touch and saccharine words a vain effort to draw me from the shadows I've chosen to inhabit.

But I recoil from her advances, from the tender concern in her eyes, for I know that I am not the polished, confident heir she thought she'd tamed.

No, I am a broken, twisted thing, a husk of my former self, and the mere thought of her gentle caress fills me with a revulsion so visceral, it leaves me reeling.

I need *Cara*, her wild beauty and uncompromising spirit - the very things that have always both terrified and enthralled me.

She is the light that has the power to cut through the all-encompassing darkness that now shrouds my every waking moment, a beacon of hope in the tempestuous sea of my own creation.

And so, I find myself gravitating towards her, like a moth irresistibly drawn to the flame, even as I know that my touch will only serve to immolate us both. I seek her out, my feet carrying me to the modest dwelling that has become her sanctuary, my heart pounding with a terrifying mix of nerves.

When she opens the door, her eyes widening with a host of unreadable emotions, I feel the last shreds of my composure crumbling. "Cara," I breathe, the name a prayer and a plea on my lips. "I need you."

But the words are hollow, devoid of the conviction and unwavering devotion that have always characterized my love for her.

For I know, deep in the marrow of my bones, that I am unworthy, a tainted, broken vessel that can offer her nothing but ruin and despair.

Cara's brow furrows, her gaze searching mine with a concern that only serves to twist the knife in my gut.

"June, what's wrong?" she asks, her voice soft and infuriatingly *kind*.

I want to crumble, to fall to my knees and beg for her forgiveness, to confess the depths of my transgressions and plead for the absolution that I know I can never truly earn.

But the words catch in my throat, strangled by the crushing weight of my shame.

Instead, I shake my head, drawing upon the last vestiges of my willpower to erect the facade of composure that has become my armor against the world.

"I'm fine," I lie, the words tasting of ash on my tongue. "I shouldn't have come. I'm sorry to have bothered you."

I turn to leave, every step a Sisyphean struggle against the tidal wave of emotions threatening to sweep me away. But Cara's hand on my arm, gentle yet unyielding, roots me to the spot.

"June, talk to me," she implores, her eyes brimming with a concern that only serves to deepen the ache in my heart. "Please, let me help you."

Help me?

The very thought is laughable, a cruel jest from a cruel universe. For how can she *help* me, when I have violated the very foundations of trust that should have been the bedrock of our relationship?

How can I burden her with the weight of my sins, when she is the only hope I have of reclaiming the shattered pieces of my soul?

"You can't," I whisper, the words laced with a sorrow so profound, it threatens to swallow me whole. "No one can."

I extricate myself from her grasp, ignoring the flicker of hurt that crosses her face, and stride away, each step a battle against the urge to turn back, to fall at her feet and beg for her forgiveness.

For I know, with a clarity that is both terrifying and absolute, that I am beyond redemption, unworthy of the light that Cara represents.

So, I retreat, burying myself once more in the trappings of my gilded cage, clinging to the false security of power and privilege as the last vestiges of my humanity slip through my grasping fingers.

And the only constant, the only *truth* , that remains is the unwavering conviction that Cara is my *salvation* - if only I can find the strength to become the man she deserves.

Chapter 11
Cara

The afternoon sun caresses my skin, a fleeting moment of warmth amidst the tempest of my emotions. Surrounded by the laughter and easy banter of Song and Louie, I feel like a ghost haunting the edges of their joy, an outsider looking in through a frosted window.

"I swear, Cara, you should've seen Grandma's face!" Song's howling laughter grates against my raw nerves, a harsh reminder of how disconnected I feel from the world around me. I force a smile, the muscles of my face straining with the effort, but it's a pale imitation of the real thing.

Sonya's hand on my arm is a lifeline, anchoring me to the present. "Cara, you okay?" Her eyes search mine, concern etched into the delicate lines of her face.

"Yeah, just thought I saw..." I trail off, shaking my head as if to dislodge the phantom image that has haunted me for weeks. Since June.

My gaze darts to the edges of the park, a compulsive habit born of equal parts fear and desperate hope. And there, like a figment of my most tortured dreams, he stands. June. Watching me with an intensity that sends shivers down my spine, a predator stalking his prey.

Panic claws at my throat, my heart a wild, caged thing beating against my ribs. I blink, and he's gone, leaving me to question the very fabric of my reality.

We decide to leave, the daylight waning into evening's softer tones. As we say our goodbyes, the lengthening shadows mirroring the growing unease that coils in my gut. Song and Louie, lost in their own blissful bubble, leave me to navigate the once-familiar paths of the park alone, as if drawn by an invisible thread of fate.

And there he is again, as solid and undeniable as the ache in my chest. June, just across the way, close enough to touch, yet a lifetime away.

I falter, my breath catching in my throat, but when I gather the courage to confront him, he melts into the gathering dusk, leaving me grasping at shadows.

The night leads me to a bar, I seek solace in the burn of alcohol and the fleeting warmth of a stranger's attention, desperate to drown out the memories that cling to me.

A guy, decent-looking and seemingly interested, slides onto the stool next to mine, offering an easy smile, and a cheesy pick-up line.

I engage, partly out of a desire to feel normal, to prove to myself I can move past the ghost of June I seem to be chasing.

But even here, in this dimly lit sanctuary, I can't escape the specter of my past. June appears like a wraith, cutting through the haze of smoke and chatter with a singular focus that steals the breath from my lungs.

"Excuse me," his voice is a cold caress, a blade slicing through the fragile illusion of normalcy I've tried to construct. "I need to speak with my wife."

Wife?

The word hangs between us, a noose tightening around my neck. The stranger beside me fades into insignificance, a bit player in the twisted drama of our lives.

June's eyes bore into mine, a challenge and a plea wrapped in one smoldering gaze. "We were just leaving, right, Cara?"

Anger and hurt propel me to my feet, a tidal wave of emotion that threatens to drag me under. "Actually, June, I wasn't. But you should." My voice is steady, but inside, I'm a hurricane.

The stranger makes his exit, and I round on June, my eyes flashing. "Why are you here?"

For a moment, he falters. "I needed to see you," he confesses, and the raw honesty tears at my defenses.

"Well, you've seen me. Happy?"

June invades my space, his proximity an assault on my senses. "Cara, please. We need to talk."

I recoil, throwing up my shields. "There's nothing left to say. You made that clear."

His composure crumbles. "Cara, I—"

"No, June!" The words pour out, each one a dagger. "You don't get to break me and then waltz back in like nothing's changed."

He takes the verbal blows, a penitent accepting his punishment. But it's not enough. It can never be enough.

"Leave, June. Leave and don't come back."

A beat. A nod. And then he's gone, leaving me in the wreckage of my emotions.

I sink back onto the stool, drained and aching, as the bartender approaches. I wave him off, the drink an empty promise of solace.

Instead, I sit alone, watching the ghost of our past disappear, feeling both shattered and strangely whole.

Outside, the night embraces me, its chill a balm to my fevered skin. Each step is a reclamation, a tiny act of defiance against the hold June has on my heart.

The days blur together, a desperate scramble for normalcy. I lose myself in work, in long walks, in the pages of books that once offered escape. But every smile is a lie, every moment of peace a betrayal of the pain that consumes me.

I throw myself into the dating scene, a frenzied search for connection, for a salve to the loneliness that gnaws at my bones. But each encounter is a bitter disappointment, a twisted mockery of the love I once knew.

There's Daniel, with his easy charm and quick wit. We arrange to meet for dinner at a cozy Italian place, and I spend hours getting ready, trying to recapture a glimmer of the confidence I once had. But as I sit at the table, minutes ticking by with no sign of him, my phone lights up with a message: "Sorry, can't make it. Something came up."

I stare at the screen, a hot flush of humiliation creeping up my neck. The waiter shoots me pitying glances as I pick at my breadsticks, trying to salvage some shred of dignity.

Then there's Ethan, with his piercing blue eyes and disarming smile. We hit it off over coffee, and he suggests a follow-up date at a trendy sushi bar. I wait outside the restaurant, my heart fluttering with nervous anticipation. Minutes stretch into an hour, and still no Ethan. My phone buzzes: "Running late, be there soon!" But soon never comes, and I'm left standing on the sidewalk, a wilting flower in a too-tight dress.

Each rejection, each no-show, is a tiny cut, a paper-thin slice into my already fragile self-esteem. I begin to wonder if there's something fundamentally wrong with me, some invisible flaw that drives people away.

The final straw comes with Dale, a manga artist who just returned from Japan. Alex, a mutual friend of June and mine, insists on setting us up. "He's perfect for you, Cara," they gush. "Creative, passionate, and he's got this quiet intensity that I think you'll love."

I'm hesitant at first, the wounds of past rejections still raw and stinging. But Alex is persistent, and I find myself agreeing to a coffee date, a tentative step back into the fray.

To my surprise, Dale and I hit it off immediately. We bond over our shared love of art, swapping stories of our creative journeys and the challenges of making it in a field that often undervalues its practitioners. He tells me about his time in Japan, the inspiration he found in the bustling streets of Tokyo and the tranquil gardens of Kyoto.

Over the next few weeks, we go on a series of dates, each one better than the last. Dale is attentive, thoughtful, and endearingly shy. He brings me sketches he's done of me, his delicate lines capturing the essence of my features in a way that makes me feel seen, appreciated.

One sunny Saturday, we plan a picnic in a private garden, a hidden oasis in the heart of the city. I spend the morning preparing an array of gourmet sandwiches and artisanal cheeses, a bottle of crisp white wine chilling in my picnic basket.

As I spread out the checkered blanket, the scent of blooming jasmine wrapping around me like a gentle hug, I feel a flicker of something I haven't felt in a long time: hope. Maybe, just maybe, Dale is different. Maybe he's the one who will finally see me, all of me, and choose to stay.

I settle onto the blanket, the minutes ticking by as I wait for Dale to arrive. Fifteen minutes pass, then thirty. I check my phone, expecting a message about running late or getting caught in traffic. But there's nothing.

An hour goes by, and the sun climbs higher in the sky, the once pleasant warmth now an oppressive heat. I pick at the food, my appetite gone, my stomach churning with a sickening mix of anxiety and dread.

And then my phone buzzes, a text lighting up the screen. My heart leaps, a momentary surge of relief. But as I read the words, my world comes crashing down around me.

"Cara, I'm sorry, but I don't think this is going to work out. We shouldn't see each other anymore. It's not you, it's me. I hope you understand."

I stare at the message, the letters blurring as hot tears fill my eyes. Not me? How can it not be me, when I'm the common denominator in all these failed connections?

I'm the one who's left waiting, always waiting, for someone to choose me, to see my worth.

With shaking hands, I pack up the untouched picnic, the once appetizing spread now a mockery of my shattered hopes. I leave the garden, the beauty of the surroundings lost on me as I trudge through the city streets, a hollowed-out shell of a woman.

That night, I find myself drawn to our old haunts, the park where June and I once whispered promises and shared dreams. I wander the paths, a ghost in a landscape of memories, until I find myself standing in front of our bench.

And there, as if summoned by the depth of my despair, is June.

I freeze, a statue carved from regret and longing. He looks up, our eyes meeting in a collision of past and present. I should walk away, should prove that I am more than the ruins he left behind.

But I am weak, and my treacherous feet carry me to him, drawn like a moth to the flame.

"June," I start, steeling myself against the tremors in my voice. "I need you to know... there was never anyone else."

A strangled laugh escapes me, a release of pent-up emotion. "I've tried to move on. God knows I've tried. But they're not you. They could never be you."

June's eyes soften, a kaleidoscope of hope and sorrow. "Cara," he breathes, my name a prayer on his lips. "It's always been you. Only you."

The confession hangs between us, a fragile bridge spanning the chasm of our mistakes. "I was a fool," he continues, his voice raw. "I was scared of how much I felt for you, of how much I still feel."

Tears prick at my eyes, hot and stinging. I step closer, drawn into his orbit. "We've both been hurt," I whisper. "We've both made mistakes. But this thing between us, it's still here. Isn't it?"

He reaches for me, tentative, as if I might shatter at his touch. I meet him halfway, our fingers tangling, a declaration of the bond we couldn't sever.

"It's here," he agrees, his voice gaining strength. "And it's worth fighting for."

I nod, a silent vow. Despite the pain, despite the scars, I am ready to leap into the unknown, to see if we can build something new from the ashes of our past.

And so, on this bench, in this park, we begin again. We talk, really talk, baring our souls and our scars in the quiet of the night. We make no grand promises, no declarations of forever. Only a commitment to try, to take each day as it comes.

When we finally stand to leave, June's arm around me feels like coming home, a piece of myself sliding back into place. I sink into his warmth, allowing myself this moment of peace amidst the uncertainty.

Walking away, hand in hand, I feel the first stirrings of hope, delicate and tentative. It's a fragile thing, this new beginning, but for the first time in longer than I can remember, I dare to believe.

In the days that follow, we relearn each other through texts and calls, each interaction a tiny step forward. June's "good morning" messages become a lifeline, a daily reminder that he's still here, still fighting for us.

Slowly, painfully, we begin to tear down the walls we've built, to confront the hurts we've inflicted and endured. It's a process that leaves us both raw and exposed, but with each confession, each moment of vulnerability, I feel the chasm between us closing.

When June suggests meeting for coffee, a flutter of nervous anticipation takes root in my stomach. This is a test, a trial by fire, to see if the fragile trust we've rebuilt can withstand the weight of proximity.

But as I step into the café and see him waiting, a calm settles over me, a bone-deep certainty that this is right, that he is right. We talk, tentative at first, feeling out the edges of our new dynamic. But slowly, like the blooming of a flower, we begin to open up, to laugh and share and simply be.

As we part ways, a promise of more hanging sweet in the air, I am suffused with warmth, a joy that I'd almost forgotten. It's a feeling of rightness, of two mismatched pieces finally fitting together.

The road ahead is long and winding, filled with untold challenges and setbacks. But we walk it together, hand in hand, hearts beating in sync. Because this, this love that refused to die, that endured through the darkest of nights, is worth every struggle, every tear, every painful step.

Chapter 12
June

The silence of my apartment is shattered by the insistent pounding on my door, each blow reverberating through my skull. I wrench it open, a snarl already curling my lips, only to find Alex's fury blazing hotter than my own.

"What the actual fuck, June?" Alex storms past me, their rage a living, breathing thing. "Threatening Dale? Have you completely lost your goddamn mind?"

My jaw clenches, a mix of shame and defiance war within me, a twisted dance of conflicting emotions. "I did what was necessary, Alex. He was encroaching on what's mine."

Alex whirls on me, their eyes twin flames of disbelief and disgust. "Yours? Cara isn't a fucking possession, June! She's a person with her own agency, her own desires. You can't just piss on her like some feral dog marking its territory!"

"She belongs with me!" The words tear from my throat, raw and bleeding. "Not with some two-bit artist who doesn't know the first thing about her!"

"Listen to yourself!" Alex's voice rises to a fever pitch. "This isn't love, it's obsession. It's sick, and it's going to destroy you both."

I stalk forward, my hands curling into fists, itching to lash out. "I don't need a lecture on love from you, Alex. What I need is for you to stay the hell out of my way."

For a moment, Alex stares at me as if I'm a stranger wearing the skin of their friend. "If you keep down this path, June, you'll lose her. You'll lose everything. Is that what you want? To be left with nothing but the ashes of your own fucked up delusions?"

Their words slice through me, the truth a serrated blade. But I can't back down, can't relinquish the obsessive need that consumes me.

"Get out, Alex. And stay away from Cara. That's not a request."

Alex lingers for a heartbeat, pity and sorrow eclipsing the anger in their eyes. "This isn't love, June. This is obsession. You're sick, and you need help."

"I don't need help," I spit, the words harsh and biting. "I need Cara. And I won't let anyone stand in my way, not even you."

For a moment, Alex looks at me as if they don't recognize me. As if the man standing before them is a stranger wearing the face of their friend.

"If you keep going down this path, June, you're going to lose her. And not just her, but everyone who cares about you. Is that what you want?"

I flinch, the truth of their words hitting me like a physical blow. But I can't back down, can't let go of the desperate, clawing need that drives me.

"Stay away from Cara, Alex. This is your final warning."

Alex lingers for a moment, sadness replacing the anger in their eyes. "I hope you find your way back, June. Before it's too late."

With that, they're gone, the sound of the door closing behind them like a gunshot in the heavy silence.

The next few days are a blur of texts and missed calls from Cara, each one a reminder of what's at stake, of what I stand to lose. We continue to talk, to rebuild something fragile yet precious, but the shadow of my secrets looms large, threatening to shatter this tentative peace we've found.

I know I need to tell her, to confess everything before the truth comes crashing down around us from other sources. But fear holds me back, fear of the look of betrayal I might see in her eyes, fear that this time, there will be no forgiveness, no second chances.

The intensity of my feelings, the chaos of my thoughts, it all builds to a breaking point. I realize that if I truly love Cara, if I truly want her in my life, I have to come clean, no matter the cost.

I'm so lost in my own spiraling thoughts that I almost miss the sound of the door opening again. For a wild, hopeful moment, I think it might be Cara.

But it's not. It's my mother, her presence as commanding and inescapable as always.

"Juniper, we need to talk," she declares, her voice cutting through the haze of my misery.

I look up at her, too drained to even attempt a facade of composure. "Mother, please. Not now."

But she's not to be deterred. "It's about the future of this family, Juniper. Your future. It can't wait."

She settles into the armchair across from me, her posture regal and unyielding. "It's time you proposed to Amethyst. It's what's expected of you."

The words hit me like a blow, driving the air from my lungs. "Mother, I can't. I don't love Amethyst. I love Cara."

Her lips thin, a telltale sign of her disapproval. "Love? What does love have to do with it? This is about duty, Juniper. About securing the Deveaux legacy."

I'm on my feet before I realize it, pacing the floor in agitation. "I can't live a lie, Mother. I can't marry someone I don't love, don't even want, just to appease some outdated sense of familial obligation."

"Don't be ridiculous, Juniper," she counters, steel in her voice. "You are the sole Deveaux heir. Your wants come second to the needs of this family."

Then she asserts with chilling finality. "Besides, it's time we ensure the continuation of our lineage. You and Amethyst will visit the doctor to discuss your... compatibility for producing heirs."

I feel like I'm suffocating, the walls of my life closing in around me. The expectations, the demands, the constant pressure to be someone I'm not - it's a weight I can no longer bear.

Her eyes flash with icy disdain. "That girl will never be one of us. She doesn't belong in our world. But Amethyst... she's a prize fit for a Deveaux heir. She'll give you children, secure our line. It's time we ensured the production of the next generation."

The walls close in around me, my vision tunneling. The expectations, the demands, the unending pressure to contort myself into a shape that will never fit - it's a yoke I can no longer bear.

"Cara is my future, Mother. My choice, my heart. Can't you see that?"

She rises, slow and regal, an empress cloaked in couture. "Willful, selfish boy. You've forgotten who you are. What you owe this family."

The laughter that spills from my lips is jagged, broken glass. "Maybe I don't want to be a Deveaux anymore. And, maybe I don't belong in our world either.."

The silence that follows is deafening. I can see the shock, the outrage in my mother's face. But beneath that, I think I see a glimmer of something else. Fear, perhaps. Or the realization that I'm no longer the compliant pawn she once could control.

"This discussion isn't over," she says finally, rising to her feet with a rustle of expensive silk. "I expect you to come to your senses, Juniper. And soon."

With that, she's gone, leaving me alone once more with the ruins of my life. I feel battered, broken, but there's a new resolve growing in the shattered spaces inside me.

I sink to the floor, my knees giving way, the weight of my choice settling on my shoulders. I feel flayed open, raw and exposed... but also, for the first time in my life, free.

I love Cara. I love her with every shattered piece of my being. And I will fight for her, for us, with every breath left in my body. Even if it means severing the strings that have made me fly all my life, cutting ties with the only world I've ever known.

My fingers tremble as I dial her number, each ring a timpani in my ears. And then, like a benediction, her voice.

"June?"

"Cara." Her name is a prayer on my lips, an invocation. "I need you. Please. There's so much I have to tell you, so much I should have said long ago."

A beat of hesitation, a held breath. Then, soft and tentative, a spark of hope. "Okay, June. I'm here."

The line goes dead, but the embers in my chest glow brighter, fanned by her words. I know the path ahead is strewn with thorns, that the wounds of our past still fester and throb. But God help me, I'll walk through fire if it means a chance to be worthy of her love.

I stumble out into the night, the city lights a blurred kaleidoscope through my tears. But for the first time in an eternity, my steps have purpose. I'm no longer a ghost drifting through the wreckage of my life - I'm a man determined to claw my way out of the darkness, to fight my way back to the light.

Back to Cara, my North Star. My savior and my absolution.

I'll lay myself bare at her feet, a sinner seeking grace. I'll confront the demons that have haunted our love, the poisonous secrets and twisted obsessions. I'll conquer my own weakness, lay waste to every rotten impulse.

And from the ashes of what we were, maybe, just maybe... we can build something new. Something pure and unbreakable.

A love forged in the crucible of our pain, tempered by the hard-won battle of every scar we've earned.

I'm halfway to Cara's place, my heart pounding in time with my frantic footsteps, when my phone vibrates in my pocket. I almost ignore it, too focused on my mission to fix what I've broken, but something compels me to check the screen.

Judith's name flashes up at me, and a sense of unease curls in my gut. She never calls this late unless it's important. I answer, my voice tight with impatience.

"Jude, I can't talk right now. I'm on my way to—"

"June, you need to come home. Right now." Her voice is strained, edged with a panic I've rarely heard from my unflappable sister. "It's an emergency."

My steps falter, torn between the pull of Cara and the urgency in Judith's tone. "What's going on?"

"It's Mother. She's arranged some sort of engagement party for you and Amethyst. June, you have to get here. This has gone too far."

My blood turns to ice in my veins, realization dawning like a cruel, twisted joke. This isn't an emergency. It's an ambush.

I storm into the mansion, my eyes immediately finding my mother's. She stands at the center of the grand foyer, a triumphant smile on her lips, Amethyst draped on her arm like a prize-winning accessory.

"What the hell is this?" I demand, my voice shaking with barely contained rage.

"Why, it's your engagement party, darling!" My mother's voice is sickly sweet, a poisoned honey. "Isn't it wonderful? Amethyst's parents and I arranged everything. We wanted it to be a surprise."

Amethyst glides over to me, slipping her hand into mine. Her touch feels wrong, a pale imitation of the electricity that sparks beneath Cara's fingertips. "Aren't you happy, June? We're finally making it official."

I wrench my hand away, disgust curling in my stomach. "I never agreed to this. I told you, Mother, I won't marry Amethyst. I love Cara."

A hush falls over the room, the gathered guests watching with bated breath, eager for the drama to unfold. My mother's eyes flash with warning, her smile turning brittle at the edges.

"Juniper, don't be ridiculous. You're just confused, that's all. Amethyst is perfect for you, can't you see that? She's your future."

"No, she's not." I step back, my heart hammering against my ribs. "Cara is my future. She's the one I want, the one I choose."

Amethyst's face crumples, tears welling in her eyes. "June, please. I love you. We're meant to be together, everyone knows it."

But I'm already shaking my head, backing away from this farce, this gilded cage masquerading as my destiny. "I'm sorry, Amethyst. But I can't live a lie. Not anymore."

I turn to leave, but my mother's voice cracks like a whip, freezing me in place. "If you walk out that door, Juniper, don't bother coming back. You'll be dead to this family, do you hear me? Dead."

For a moment, I waver, the weight of her words settling like lead in my chest. To be cast out, cut off from the only life I've ever known… it's a terrifying prospect.

But then I think of Cara, of her smile, her laugh, the way she makes me feel like I can breathe for the first time in my life. And I know, with a bone-deep certainty, that she's worth any price, any sacrifice.

"Then I guess this is goodbye, Mother." My voice is steady, resolved. "I choose Cara. I choose love. And if that makes me dead to you, then so be it."

I walk out, my head held high, leaving behind the shattered remains of my old life. But as I step outside, the heavens open up, a torrential downpour engulfing the world around me.

The rain lashes against my skin, cold and unforgiving, as if the very sky is weeping for the choices I've made, the pain I've caused. I race to my car, my fingers slipping on the wet handle as I wrench the door open. The engine roars to life, and I peel out onto the street, the tires hydroplaning on the slick asphalt.

Fat raindrops floods my vision, a relentless assault that mirrors the tempest raging in my heart. I can barely see the road ahead, but I don't slow down.

I can't. Nothing will stop me from getting to my Cara Mia.

Every second I waste is another second Cara is without my love...my undying devotion.

I grip the steering wheel until my knuckles turn white, my jaw clenched so tight it aches. Prayers and curses spill from my lips in equal measure, desperate pleas to a god I'm not sure I believe in anymore.

I pull out my phone with trembling fingers, my heart in my throat as I dial Cara's number. It rings once, twice, three times... and then goes to voicemail.

"Cara, it's me." My voice is raw, barely recognizable over the roar of the rain. "I'm coming to you. I'm choosing you, do you hear me? I love you, and I'm going to fight for us. For our future. Just... just wait for me, okay? I'll be there soon."

Please, God, let her be at home.

The prayer echoes in my mind, a desperate mantra that drowns out all other thoughts. I can't bear the thought of Cara in another man's arms...of him tainting her with his vile touch. My heart is a jackhammer in my chest, each beat a frantic chant of her name.

Cara. Cara. Cara.

I have to get to her. I *have* to. Losing her is not an option, not when I'm finally ready to fight for what's ours. For the love we've both been too stubborn, too afraid, to fully embrace.

The car careens around a corner, tires squealing, and I curse under my breath. I'm so close, I can *feel* it. But what if I'm too late? What if I've already lost her?

The very thought steals the breath from my lungs, leaving me gasping. No, I can't think like that. I *won't*.

All that matters is Cara. My Cara Mia. And I'll be damned if I let anyone, *anything*, stand in my way.

But as I round the corner to her street, I skid to a halt, my blood turning to ice in my veins. There, parked outside her building, is a familiar sleek black car, my father's car.

And leaning against it, a smirk twisting his lips, is a face I hoped never to see again.

Ray.

Cara's ex.

The man who nearly destroyed her.

Chapter 13
Cara

The city's pulse thrums through my veins as I navigate the neon-drenched streets, the day's trials clinging to me like a second skin. As I round the corner, my sanctuary in sight, I freeze, my blood turning to ice.

There, on my doorstep, a tableau ripped from my darkest nightmares - and the two men who broke my heart.

Ray, at the mercy of June's unleashed fury. Shock, fear, and a twisted sense of righteous vindication wage war within me as I watch June exact his brutal vengeance.

"This is for Cara, you fucking bastard!" June's voice is a guttural roar, each word punctuated by a sickening crack of flesh on flesh. "For every goddamn piece of her you left shattered in my hands!"

Ray's broken form crumples, a macabre marionette with its strings cut, and a dark, primal part of me revels in his agony. The bitter tang of copper fills the air, a heady elixir that sets my heart racing. He deserves this, I think, my lips curling into a feral snarl. He deserves to bleed, to suffer, as I did.

But even as I savor this moment of karmic retribution, the rational corner of my mind rebels. This path, drenched in blood and rage, leads only to ruin. I can't let June lose himself to the abyss, can't let him sacrifice his soul on the altar of my vengeance.

"June, enough!" My voice cracks like a whip, sharp and commanding. "He's not worth it."

June stills, his chest heaving, eyes wild and unfocused. He turns to me, a maelstrom of emotions playing across his blood-spattered face - desperation, anguish, and a bone-deep hunger that sends a shiver racing down my spine. But beneath the chaos, a spark of recognition, a silent plea for absolution.

"Cara," he rasps, my name a benediction on his lips, salvation and damnation in one breath. "You came."

I step forward, palm outstretched, a gesture of supplication. "I'm here, June. But this" - I sweep my hand towards Ray's whimpering husk - "this won't fix what's broken."

Defiance flares in June's eyes, bright and unyielding. "He destroyed you, Cara. Fuck, he nearly ended you. I won't let that stand."

My chest constricts, a vice of unspoken anguish. "I know, June. God, do I know." My words are a broken whisper, raw and bleeding. "But this... this will only destroy you, too."

The fight drains from him, shoulders slumping in weary resignation. With a last, disgusted glance at Ray, June hauls him up, fingers biting into mottled flesh.

"Crawl back to whatever hole you slithered out of," June hisses, venom dripping from every word. "And if I ever catch you near Cara again, I'll rip out your fucking throat."

Ray staggers into the night, a broken phantom, as June watches, jaw clenched and eyes haunted. He turns to me, a man laid bare, stripped of all pretense.

"Cara, fuck, I'm so sorry. For all of it."

I close the distance between us, my touch a whispered absolution as I cradle his face. "I know, June. I know."

In the fractured light, I see the boy I fell for, the man I lost myself to - flawed and fierce, tender and terrifying. The man who, despite every scar and sin, fights with all he is to be what I need.

"I've fucked everything up," he says, his brow pressed to mine, breath mingling in the scant space between us. "I'm not worthy of your forgiveness, but Christ, Cara, it's all I want. All I'll ever want."

His words, raw and aching, pierce through the armor I've spent so long crafting. Without hesitation, I pull him to me.

"I know, June." I whisper, the words a meager attempt at comfort. "I know."

June's eyes shimmer with unshed tears, as the words keep spilling out.

"I've made such a mess of things," he murmurs, his forehead coming to rest against mine. "I've hurt you, betrayed your trust. I don't deserve you, but God, Cara, I *want* you. I *need* your love, more than I've ever needed anything."

The raw vulnerability in his voice tugs at my heartstrings, a fragile thread of connection I thought I'd severed for good as the last of his composure crumbles.

"We'll get through this, June," I murmur, my fingers threading through his hair, a lifeline in the tempest. "But no more hiding. It's just us now, all the way."

His arms tighten around me, a drowning man clinging to salvation. "Anything, Cara. Everything. Just don't let go."

The broken desperation in his plea splinters something deep within me. Even with the ruins of our love scattered at our feet, the embers of what we once had, what we could be again, refuse to die.

"I'm not going anywhere," I breathe, lips pressed to his temple, a vow seared into skin and soul.

We remain locked in our embrace, twin hearts beating out a fragile hymn of hope amidst the gathering shadows. The ghosts of our sins linger, but in the shelter of each other's arms, the promise of absolution gleams.

Reluctantly, we untangle our limbs, eyes meeting in a profound sort of silence. The shattered pieces of our story lie between us, waiting to be reassembled.

"Stay with me tonight?" The question is soft, laced with cautious yearning. "I think we have some long overdue conversations ahead of us."

June nods, a flicker of apprehension crossing his features. But beneath it, I see a renewed determination, a man resolved to face the consequences of his actions.

As we step into the apartment, the air feels charged, heavy with the unspoken words that linger between us. But there's also a sense of possibility, a glimmer of light in the darkness that has threatened to consume us both.

This is merely the beginning of a new chapter, one that will probably test the very limits of our love and resilience.

A few days later, I find myself entranced, watching the video play on mute. It's probably not healthy, this urge to keep tabs on him—yet, this is the thirtieth loop.

I can't help it; These glimpses into his life, they're like a band-aid on a bullet wound barely filling the void his absence creates .

In the footage, June and his sister Judith are perched on a sailboat, their hair caught in a wild dance by the wind. Despite the chaos around them, June exudes a sense of calm and strength.

His muscular arms are visible, a huge difference to Judith's slender frame, yet both seem at home...but whenever they were together, June is always like this. There was nothing in this world that could change the way June loves his big sister.

But what draws my gaze most is a small detail: a tattoo of the letter C, elegantly scripted just below June's ribs clear on the taut contours of his abdomen. It's a simple mark, yet it speaks volumes.

My breath catches in my throat, a deep sense of longing washing over me. I want nothing more than to reach out and touch his tattoo, to feel the raised ink against my fingertips. But I resist the urge, knowing that doing so would only complicate things further.

Juniper Deveaux hated the idea of a tattoo before, but now that I see it, I can't help but wonder about the significance behind it.

Is it a tribute to me?

I want to know more, to uncover the secrets that lie beneath his skin. I want him to live in me, create with me. Fill my womb with his seed and brand me with his essence.

It's like our souls are intertwined, and no matter how far apart we are, I can feel him.

And yet, part of me is still hesitant. What if he doesn't feel the same way? What if I'm just fooling myself into thinking that our bond is real?

But then I remember the tattoo, the single letter "C" that he has etched into his skin. It's a symbol, a mark that says he belongs to me - or maybe it's the other way around. Either way, it gives me hope.

I let out a shuddering breath, my fingers continuing their descent as I imagine June's strong arms wrapping around me, his lips pressing against mine. I can feel his breath on my skin, his body pressed against me as we make love.

As my fingers touch the fabric of my pants, I imagine June's skilled hands guiding me, exploring every inch of my body. I close my eyes and let my mind wander, immersing myself in the fantasy of him loving me.

A soft moan escapes my lips as I let go of all my inhibitions, lost in the lustful thoughts. Images of us making a family, of June's touch, of his love – it's all consuming.

My body shakes with pleasure, I can't help but wonder - is this what June feels for me? This overwhelming need, this all-encompassing love? I can't help but think that maybe, just maybe, our souls were made for each other.

And as I lie in bed, the sweat drying on my skin, I know that I'll do whatever it takes to be with him.

It's not long before, I find myself back at our favorite coffee shop, trying to ignore the persistent butterflies in my stomach. I've summoned June here under the pretense of discussing our next steps, but the real reason for this meetup is bubbling just beneath the surface - a temptation I've been wrestling with for far too long.

As if summoned by my thoughts, June arrives.

Our eyes meet, a collision of want and wariness, the crackle of a connection never severed, only dormant.

"June." My voice is steady, even as my heart threatens to beat out of my chest. "We need to talk."

Concern etches itself across his brow. "Anything, Cara. I'm here."

A shaky inhale, a steadying exhale. "What if... what if we tried something new? Something different this time?"

His head tilts, curiosity warring with trepidation in his gaze. "Different how?"

"Friends," I say, the word feeling foreign on my tongue. "Friends with... benefits."

Shock ripples across June's features, quickly replaced by something darker, hungrier. "Benefits?" he echoes, the ghost of a smirk playing at the corner of his mouth.

I nod, holding his gaze with a boldness I barely feel. "No commitments, no demands. Just two people, finding solace in each other."

The air between us crackles with barely restrained tension, the weight of unspoken desires hanging heavy. June's eyes rake over me, a touch in itself, igniting every nerve ending with the promise of primal indulgence.

"Well then, my Cara Mia," he purrs, voice dripping with seductive menace, "lead the way."

Powerless to resist the pull, I grasp his hand, letting pure instinct guide me. We crash through the door, all desperate hands and greedy mouths, our bodies tangling in a frenzied dance of lust and longing.

June presses me against the wall, his hardness searing into my yielding curves, his tongue plundering the depths of my mouth until I'm dizzy from lack of oxygen.

"Tell me what you need," he commands, growling against the fevered skin of my throat. His fingers dance along my hem, teasing, pushing the boundaries of control.

"You," I pant, arching shamelessly into him. "I need you to erase every trace of your absence, claim me so completely that I forget I was ever shattered."

Something fierce and feral ignites in June's eyes, a man possessed. "As my queen commands," he rumbles, a vow and a warning.

June's eyes flash, a man possessed. "As my queen commands," he rumbles, a dark oath against my lips.

He moves to undo my skirt, and I feel the cool air on my bare thighs. He looks up at me, a fierce heat burning in his eyes.

"Are you sure?" he asks, his voice low and rough.

"I've never been more sure of anything in my life," I whisper, my heart pounding in my chest.

There is only us...only this moment - the explosive collision of two damaged souls finally fusing back together. June worships my body with hands and mouth, relearning every curve and hollow, stoking the flames until I am molten beneath his touch.

When he finally takes me, the pleasure borders on pain, raw and visceral and utterly consuming. I cry out his name like a prayer, nails carving half-moons into his sweat-slicked skin as he drives into me again and again, a relentless claiming.

Beyond these walls, the aftermath of my revenge and the uncertain future loom. But here, cocooned in the scorching sanctuary of June's embrace, the shattered pieces of my heart slowly begin to realign.

This is more than base desire, more than a bandage over still-bleeding wounds.

It is absolution and reckoning, a sacrament of broken souls finding solace in the only place they've ever truly belonged - with each other.

"Do you like that?" he growls into my ear, his warm breath sending tingles through every nerve ending in my body.

I moan softly, unable to resist the intense desire coursing through my veins. "Yes," I whisper, feeling a rush of pleasure spread through every inch of my being.

June's hand moves from my hip to the small of my back, pushing me even closer against his hardened length. With a swift movement, he lifts me up and pins me against the wall of the alleyway, trapping me there with his body heat and muscular frame.

"You're mine tonight," he murmurs huskily into my ear, his hot breath making me shiver with anticipation.

I can feel the power dynamics shift between us as he takes control of our encounter. It's intoxicating; I've never felt so desired or so submissive before. I bite my lip nervously, unsure of what is going to happen next but knowing that I am willing to go wherever he leads me.

His lips move towards mine, claiming them in a passionate kiss that leaves me breathless and wanting more. His tongue dances with mine, teasing and taunting until I feel myself melting against him like warm honey on a hot summer day.

As we break apart for air, our eyes lock onto each other's like two predators sizing up their prey. I can feel myself getting wetter by the second just from looking at him. He smiles wickedly at this realization before lowering himself back down onto his knees between my legs once again.

Without warning, he parts my folds with his fingers and thrusts two fingers deep inside of my pussy while simultaneously sucking on one of my nipples through the fabric of my dress.

The dual sensations are too much for me to handle; I cry out loudly as waves upon waves of pleasure crash over my body like an ocean tide coming ashore during a stormy night.

"Fuck," he growls out between clenched teeth. "I'm going to make you come so hard your legs will shake."

With that, June begins moving his fingers inside me faster, each thrust causing a new wave of pleasure to wash over me. My breaths become shallow and ragged, my moans filling the alley as his mouth works its magic on my nipple.

"Is that what you want?" he asks, his voice low and husky.

I nod wildly, unable to speak coherently through my building orgasm.

He pulls away from my nipple and looks up at me, his eyes blazing with lust.

"You're going to cum for me, Cara. You're going to scream my name and let go of every last bit of control you've been holding on to."

I can't help but nod again, my eyes locked with June's as I prepare for the most intense orgasm of my life.

He increases his pace, thrusting his fingers deeper and harder into my pussy until I can no longer hold back. I cry out his name, arching my back and writhing under his touch as wave after wave of pleasure washes over me.

"That's it, my Cara Mia. Be a good girl and cum for me," June demands, his voice hoarse with desire. "Let go and let me take you."

And I do.

I let go of every last bit of control I have left, screaming his name as I come harder than I ever thought possible.

Still, June continues to thrust his fingers into me until the last shuddering wave has passed, leaving me panting and spent. I groan softly as his fingers slowly withdraw from the intimate space, my body still pulsing with the echoes of pleasure.

Then, June brushes his fingers against my lips, his gaze dark and intense as he looks down at me. "Damn," he murmurs.

I struggle to steady my breath, my chest rising and falling rapidly as he leans in to capture my lips in a searing kiss. Our breaths meld in the cool night air, a symphony of heat and need as his tongue dances against my parted lips.

Fingers tangle in my hair, a gentle tug adding electricity to the already charged moment. Breaking away with a low groan, he extends a hand to help me up.

And like the greedy whore I am... my body already wants more of his touch.

"Get dressed," June's voice is rough with command as he assists me to my feet. "We're just getting started."

The thrill of pleasure and exhaustion swirls within me as I inhale deeply the crisp night breeze. I gaze at him quizzically, but all I receive in response is a smirk before he disappears into the shadows between the trees.

My heart races, unable to shake off the waves of desire pushing me further.

The fabric against my skin is both comforting and maddening, heightening my senses. Thoughts swirl in my mind, envisioning what thrilling escapade might unfold next.

It seems almost impossible for tonight to become any more intense than it already is.

Chapter 14
June

I stare at the computer screen, my fingers hovering over the keyboard, poised to sever the last thread connecting me to Cara's world. With each keystroke, I'm erasing the silent, voyeuristic link that's kept me tethered to her life - a twisted lifeline in the tempestuous sea of my existence without her.

There's a sense of relief in this action, a recognition that I'm finally putting right what was inherently wrong. But the ache of loss is impossible to ignore. This digital window, as unhealthy as it was, has been my only connection to Cara.

I'm about to delete the final surveillance files when Scott bursts in, his presence more unsettling than comforting. My heart pounds, a silent prayer that Cara's friendship with Louis is as innocent as she claims. But the nagging doubt persists, especially in the harsh light of the revelations I'm about to face.

"June," Scott begins, his voice devoid of pleasantries, "I've got some new information on Cara and Louis."

I lean forward, my pulse quickening. "What is it?"

"They're spending a lot of time together outside of work," Scott reveals, his tone clinical yet loaded. "And recently, while shadowing Cara, I overheard them discussing a trip. They're planning to go out of town together, for a week or more."

A week. The words echo in my mind, a relentless drumbeat. Jealousy, that toxic companion, grips me hard, painting vivid images of Cara and Louis, laughing, exploring, sharing intimate moments that should be mine.

Especially now, when Cara and I have finally crossed that line, blurring the boundaries between friendship and something more. The memory of her skin against mine, the taste of her lips, the sounds of our shared pleasure - it all comes rushing back, a tidal wave of sensations that leaves me reeling.

How can she plan a trip with another man, when just days ago, she was in my arms, begging me to erase every trace of my absence from her body and soul?

"Are you sure?" I demand, my voice strained, barely recognizing the possessive edge to my words.

Scott nods. "I confirmed it in Louis' bank records. He paid for the tickets and a reservation at an Airbnb."

I push away from the window, my anger barely masking the trembling in my limbs. The room suddenly feels too small, the walls closing in around me as the implications of Scott's words sink in.

"Anything else?"

"That's all I have for now, June. I'm sorry."

"Thanks, Scott," I manage, my voice hollow. He nods, casting me a sympathetic look before leaving, the door clicking shut behind him.

The deafening silence hangs like a vise around my throat as I sink into the buttery leather chair behind my desk. Its unyielding embrace is a cruel reminder that I am utterly and hopelessly alone in this hell of my own creation.

My hand trembles, almost of its own accord, as I snatch up my phone and dial Judith's number. I need her - my lifeline, my last tether to reality amid the maelstrom decimating what little sanity I have left.

The phone barely rings once before she answers, her voice a soothing balm that does little to ease the eternal burn.

"June? What's wrong?"

I open my mouth, but the words refuse to come. All I can expel is a primordial sound of anguish - a wounded animal's cry.

"Junie, talk to me. You're scaring me."

And that's what finally breaks the dam. A torrent of rage and sorrow, of bitter jealousy and searing shame, comes pouring out in a frenzy.

"How could she, Jude? How could she do this to me?" Each question is punctuated by a fresh wave of torment crashing over me.

"She was mine. MINE. After everything, after laying my soul bare...she's going to run away with HIM!" The roar that rips from my chest would be feral if it carried any less desolation.

Judith tries to reason with me, to instill some fragile sense of calm and rationality. But her words are a mere whisper against the howling gale of my emotions.

White-hot fury lances through me, an explosive bloom of lava incinerating any shred of coherence. I lash out, words becoming indiscriminate weapons - each syllable a serrated blade aimed at inflicting maximum carnage.

I can almost see them piercing Judith, her sharp inhales of shock and hurt like blood in the water. But in my crazed, consuming spiral, her pain only fuels my destructive tailspin further.

Horrible, unforgivable things leave my lips, vile shapes accusing her of being against me, of siding with that insignificant worm actively trying to steal away the only light in my bleak existence.

When at last I've fully expended the molten rage, I'm left hollowed out and seared from the inside. A charred ruin amid the ashes of what was once a deep, abiding love between siblings.

"June…" Judith's voice is wet and gravelly, sloshing with watery tears. "I can't…I can't do this anymore. Not until you get help. Until you stop—-"

The line goes dead before she can unleash the killing blow. Beneath the crackling static, I can hear it anyway - the whispers accusing me of utter madness, of being a complete and irredeemable monster.

As the scorpion's cage slams shut around me, I'm vaguely aware of muted footsteps approaching. In my shattered delirium, I almost expect a SWAT team to burst in, prepared to put down this rabid dog before I can infect anyone else.

Instead, it's Amethyst who materializes before me, looking uncharacteristically small in the elongated shadows of my ruination. I barely register the trepidation in her eyes as she hovers in the doorway like a startled bird assessing the wisdom of entering this viper's nest.

"June?" Her voice is barely above a breath, as if speaking too loudly might shatter the fragile detente. "Are…are you alright?"

The concern on her face, so sincere yet so wildly misplaced, almost splits the hairline fractures in my sanity wide open again. A harsh, barking rasp of bitter laughter explodes from the ruin of my throat.

"Alright?" My lips peel back in a cutting sneer as I regard this woman - this girl playing at having any comprehension of my anguish. "Didn't you hear, love? The world is ending. Again. And this time, I'm the harbinger."

I stalk towards her, each footfall carrying the weight of the world I'm no longer welcome in. A panther advancing on a trembling lamb, knowing full well it has invited slaughter.

When I reach her, I can't help but drink in the details - the fluttering pulse in her throat, the rapid dilating of her pupils, the sweet, heady scent of trepidation and adrenaline. It's intoxicating in a sickly, mocking sort of way.

Leaning in with excruciating slowness, I let my lips brush the delicate whorls of her ear as I murmur, "You should run, little bird. Before the Big Bad Wolf decides he's forgotten how to play nice."

She moves closer, her heels clicking against the floor. "I just wanted to check on you."

Irritation flares within me, white-hot. "Didn't I make myself clear at the mansion? I don't want you, Amethyst. I will never want you."

She flinches, hurt flickering in her eyes. "June, I'm just trying to be here for you."

"Wasn't it clear, Amethyst?" I snap, the words like venom. "Just buy a fucking clue with my mother's money and leave me the hell alone. Christ?"

I can feel her recoil in reticent horror, but I pay it no mind. I'm far too fascinated watching the war between indoctrinated politeness and self-preservation play out across her delicate features.

When at last she retreats, it's with a thin veneer of composure barely restraining the instinctive flight of prey leaving the presence of an apex predator. The door closes with shaking finality behind her.

In the echoing silence that follows, I'm left feeling...nothing. No guilt, no sense of shame or regret. Just a vast, empty crater where Cara's brilliance used to reside, leaving me drifting in the cosmic void of loss.

Sinking back into my chair, I let the visions of her play on a loop behind my eyes - her smiles, her laugh, the cascading rivulets of pleasure that used to grace her features when I worshiped her body.

I need to burn those memories into my ruined psyche. Let them scar me down to the very marrow. Because very soon, I know those precious few recollections will be all I have left of her radiance before she's gone.

Spirited away by that grinning pretender, that pathetic excuse for a man who fancies himself worthy of claiming what was always, is always, MINE.

The possessive snarl that rips up from my core would be terrifying if it didn't bring with it a tantalizing new shard of purpose, or retribution. My Cara will not be stolen, not while there's still breath in my body to fight.

I'll tear this world asunder and rebuild it in her image if that's what it takes to reclaim what is rightfully mine.

When my lips claim hers once more, it will be a conquering - a reminder to herself as much as that guttersnipe grifter of who her seared soul truly belongs to. I'll kiss her until she's breathless, senseless, consumed by the fire she awoke.

My hands curl into claws, nails biting crescents into my palms until I taste the copper kiss of my own blood on my lips. The pain is a welcome respite, a purifying lash keeping me anchored to reality, to the hunt now stretching out before me.

I am the wolf in these woods, and no helpless lamb will outrun me. Not on my trail, not when the prize is the only thing giving my decrepit existence purpose anymore. Cara is my wonderland, and unlike that golden-haired bitch of lore, I've no intention of ever leaving.

Let that soulless puppet attempt to whisk her away from me. I'll merely be waiting, a rabid Minotaur ready to consume anyone who dares trespass on my sacred hunt for her essence.

Ruin will be their judgment, and by the blackened time I'm finished, they'll be grateful for something as merciful as mere death. I'll baptize them in the fires that have consumed my humanity, immolating their very existence from reality.

Only then, when the ashes of their arrogance are scattered to the void, will I pull Cara back in to taste the truth - that she is the Dark

Phoenix to my Oblivion, and our real Scorched Earth is only just beginning.

Cara's impending journey with Louis gnaws at me like a relentless tide, eroding the fragile facade of composure I've painstakingly constructed. The mere thought of her in his arms, sharing moments that should rightfully be ours, twists like a knife in my gut, a constant torment I can scarcely bear.

In the days that ensue, I become a phantom, haunting the periphery of her life. I stalk her every move, a silent predator observing its prey, waiting for the perfect moment to strike. The comic convention is my hunting ground, a labyrinth of costumed revelry where I can blend into the shadows, unseen and unnoticed.

I watch her from afar, drinking in every detail - the way her eyes light up when she spots a rare comic, the musical lilt of her laughter as she banters with fellow enthusiasts. She's a vision of joy and innocence, a stark contrast to the darkness festering within me.

But even in the midst of this colorful chaos, my eyes are drawn to him - to Louis, the interloper who dares to bask in her radiance. They move through the convention together, shoulders brushing, smiles traded like precious currency. Each casual touch is a dagger to my gut, a vivid reminder of what I stand to lose.

It takes every ounce of my fraying self-control not to lunge forward, to rip her away from his unworthy grasp and claim her as my own before the entire world. But I force myself to remain still, to blend into the background like a wraith, biding my time.

The true test of my restraint comes later, at the convention's after-party. The club is a pulsing, neon-drenched den of hedonism, the bass throbbing like a second heartbeat. And there, in the center of the dance floor, are Cara and Louis, their bodies entwined in a sensual rhythm that makes my blood boil.

I watch, transfixed and seething, as his hands roam over her curves, as she grinds against him with wanton abandon. The primal, possessive beast within me roars to life, demanding that I storm the dance floor and assert my claim, consequences be damned.

But through the red haze of my fury, a single thought crystallizes - Cara. Her happiness, her trust, the fragile bond we've only just begun to rebuild. If I lose control now, if I let the monster win, I risk losing her forever.

So I force myself to turn away, to melt back into the shadows, my nails digging bloody crescents into my palms. Every step away from her is an agony, a visceral tearing at the very fabric of my being. But I endure it, for her.

In the alleyway behind the club, I unleash my anguish, my fists pummeling the unyielding brick until my knuckles are raw and bleeding. The physical pain is a welcome distraction, a way to ground myself in the here and now, to keep the beast at bay.

But even as I compose myself, straightening my collar and smoothing my hair, I know this reprieve is only temporary. The war for Cara's heart is far from over, and I will stop at nothing to emerge victorious.

I may have lost this battle, but the war rages on. And in the end, I know with unshakable certainty that she will be mine - wholly, irrevocably, eternally.

No matter the cost, no matter the ruin left in my wake, I will fight for her until my dying breath. Because a world without Cara is no world at all.

So I retreat into the night, a predator licking his wounds, plotting his next move. Louis may have won this round, but he has no idea of the hell that awaits him.

For I am Juniper Deveaux, and when it comes to Cara, there is no length I won't go to, no line I won't cross, to make her mine once more.

The game has only just begun, and I play for keeps.

Chapter 15
Cara

San Diego's perpetual sunshine does little to warm the chill that's taken up residence in my bones. I huddle deeper into my jacket as I navigate the bustling streets, the clamor of Comic-Con fever swirling all around me.

Normally, being surrounded by such vibrant celebrations of creativity and fandom would fill me with anticipation. But today, it all feels muted, as if I'm viewing the world through a grimy pane of glass separating me from the vibrancy.

Maybe it's the lingering exhaustion from the cross-country trip. Or the unshakable sense that I'm being watched, studied, hunted. My hand clenches reflexively in my pocket, fingers brushing against the small canister of pepper spray that has become my constant companion.

Get a grip, Cara. You're just being paranoid.

Louis's familiar laughter cuts through the din, and I pivot instinctively toward the sound. He's standing outside a trendy cafe, all effortless charm in a fitted suit as he chats with a stunning blonde woman. For a moment, the sight fills me with an irrational flare of something acidic—jealousy? dismay? Loneliness?

Thoughts of June fills my mind, and I find myself missing him...missing his touch.

Then Louis spots me and that signature smile, the one that could melt glaciers, stretches across his face. With a gentle hand on the small of the blonde's back, he guides her toward me.

"Cara! You're never going to believe who I just ran into."

Before I can react, he sweeps me up in one of his trademark hugs, all warmth and solid reassurance.

My cheek grazes his lapel, and I inhale the intoxicating blend of his cologne and the faint traces of cedar and carnations that is uniquely Louis.

Instantly, the chill recedes, if only for a moment. Being wrapped in Louis's embrace is like sinking into the comforting familiarity of a favorite sweater. Safe, secure, something to be savored until it inevitably slips from your shoulders.

All too soon, he releases me, though his hands linger on my shoulders as he pivots to make the introduction.

"Cara, I'd like you to meet my niece, Bianca. Bianca, this is Cara, the remarkable artist I've been telling you about."

Bianca gives me a warm smile, all polished beauty and understated wealth. Up close, it's apparent she and Louis share the same striking eyes, the same regal bone structure that seems to mark them as members of some nigh-untouchable aristocracy.

"It's so wonderful to finally meet you, Cara." Her voice is lilting and melodic, cultured without being affected. "Louis speaks of you so fondly, I feel as if I know you already."

There's a knowing glint in Louis's eyes as they meet mine, a silent acknowledgment that he's been waxing poetic about my virtues once again. I shoot him a playful glare, but I can't quite keep the grin from tugging at my lips.

"Is that so?" I arch an eyebrow at him. "I'd ask what kind of stories he's been telling, but knowing Louis, they're probably too scandalous for polite company."

Louis clutches his chest in an exaggerated show of mock indignation. "Why, Cara! I'm wounded that you'd impugn my honor in such a brazen manner." He turns to his niece, all teasing levity. "This is the thanks I get for simply celebrating the boundless talents of my dearest friend."

Bianca laughs, the sound like a tinkling crystal chime. "Yes, well, if the stories are anything like the ones I grew up hearing about you, dear uncle, I can only imagine."

Their banter is easy, the kind of effortless rapport that speaks of a bond forged in equal parts deep affection and gentle needling. I can't help but feel a fleeting pang at being on the outside of that intimacy looking in.

But then Louis's arm drapes casually across my shoulders, and the chill that had been whispering through my mind goes utterly still and silent.

"So, Cara, I was just filling Bianca in on the main reason for my extended stay." The arm around me squeezes lightly, a comforting anchor. "My plan to spend some quality time getting to know my delightful niece a bit better, seeing as a certain scamp barely lets me visit anymore."

Bianca lets out a long-suffering sigh far too theatric to be sincere. "Uncle Louis, you know that's not true at all. I'm simply trying to give you space to focus on the extraordinary, globe-spanning adventures that make up your daily life as an elite international art courier."

There's an impish glint in her eyes, one I've seen countless times when Louis and I are winding each other up. Clearly, the teasing, affectionate banter is a family trait they both relish in.

"Yes, well," Louis continues, his tone drier than the Sahara, "whatever mundane duties I may occasionally engage in pale in comparison to your roles as both philanthropic socialite and pearl of the western catalytic heritage scene."

I feel a surprised laugh bubbling up from somewhere deep in my chest. Only Louis could make even the most banal exchanges seem like excerpts from the world's most deliciously worded comic drama.

In that moment, some of the weight I've been carrying seems to lift ever so slightly. The tension leaches from my shoulders as I take in the warm familiarity of Louis and his childhood friends' easy rapport.

This, here, is the kind of uncomplicated affection and acceptance that has been in such short supply lately.

"Well," I chime in, giving Louis's arm a playful jab with my elbow, "we all can't be ridiculously wealthy and well-connected art dealers, now can we? Some of us poors have to make do slumming it in the creative gutter, trading our souls to the comic book ninja assassins one paneled page at a time."

Louis's eyes crease with mirth, and I realize just how long it's been since I've allowed myself to simply...breathe. To lean into the easy camaraderie of friends and revel in the safety of companionship without agenda or expectation.

But the moment, as all too many seem to lately, is fleeting.

From the corner of my eye, I catch a glimpse of movement - a tall, imposing figure in a dark suit and mirrored shades weaving through the crowd. My pulse kicks up a frantic staccato as something primal and instinctual sets every nerve afire.

Without conscious thought, I move closer to Louis, pressing into his side like a flower leaning toward the sun. Louis might be my best friend, but he's no June.

His hand squeezes my shoulder, a silent question jarred from its path by the way my entire body tenses like a tripwire.

I shake my head minutely, just once. A clear signal not to draw attention, not to make a scene. He nods, the slightest dip of his chin to show he understands my meaning.

Turning to Bianca, he flashes his most devastating grin, the one that never fails to melt any resistance in its path.

"Well, my dear, what say we make our way inside? I have it on good authority the barista here was trained by Tibetan monks to imbue each drop of coffee with the life-altering power of transcendent clarity."

Bianca arches an elegant brow at her uncle but allows herself to be swept up in his charismatic wake with what is clearly long-practiced ease. I follow, keeping their bodies between me and the street as much as possible while fighting to control my hammering heart.

The cafe is blessedly cool, a soothing oasis that allows me to draw a stabilizing breath. As we stake out a plush corner booth, hemmed in on all sides, I finally allow some of the panicked tension to ebb.

"Alright there, darling?" Louis asks, voice pitched low. He settles in next to me, shielding me from the room while keeping the retreat paths clear. An unconscious exploitation of tactical positioning that speaks to deeper currents lurking beneath his suave, easygoing exterior.

"I...yeah. Yeah, I'm fine." The lie feels leaden on my tongue, but I can't quite bring myself to shatter the illusion of normalcy just yet. "Just a long couple of days, I suppose."

He narrows those arresting green eyes at me, letting the silence spill just long enough to make it clear he's not buying my deflection for a second. I huff out a resigned breath, slumping ever so slightly against his solid frame.

"Later," I murmur, knowing any further evasion is an exercise in futility. He knows I have a stalker and leaving me open to danger was the last thing on his mind.

Louis nods, wordless understanding and acceptance. Out of the corner of my eye, I catch Bianca studying us both with an unreadable expression.

The moment passes, like so many others. The three of us slip into the effortless rhythms of banter and conversation, seamlessly weaving in Bianca as if she's been part of our dynamic all along.

Watching the easy way Louis and his niece interact, the genuine warmth and affection that shines through their every interaction. I am happy for my friend. He's looked for acceptance for so long, and with all he does for everyone else.

It's something that now, more than ever, I know he needs.

When at last the endless hours of travel catch up to me, it takes very little effort to let Louis herd me toward the discreet town car idling out front. Bianca gives me a warm farewell, pressing a soft kiss to each of my cheeks in a way that feels so earnestly affectionate I nearly forget how to breathe.

"Until next time, dear Cara," she murmurs, those striking eyes filled with a sincerity that tugs at my heart.

I manage a smile and a small nod, the lump in my throat too thick for words. She turns, all effortless elegance and affluent grace as she drifts away into the San Diego night.

Beside me, Louis radiates a bittersweet aura, like a devoted son forced to watch his child strike out on their own. There's an ancient pride there, one he clearly takes great pains to conceal behind his characteristic unflappable composure.

"She's extraordinary, isn't she?" The wistful words slip from his lips in a hushed murmur, more an exhalation of paternal awe than any need for validation.

"Yes," I answer just as quietly, understanding on a bone-deep level that this isn't a moment for noisy grandstanding. "Yes, she really is."

The ghost of a melancholic smile plays over his features before the mask of urbane inscrutability descends once more. Tucking my hand securely into the crook of his elbow, he guides me toward the waiting car.

Once inside, I can't quite stifle the groan of relief as I sink into the plush leather seat. Like an overstuffed body settling into a perfectly tailored impression, the whispers of the outside world finally fade into irrelevance.

Louis slides in alongside me, the heavy door thudding shut and cutting off the last tendrils of the city's raucous symphony. We sit for a long stretch in that casually contented silence that so few others in the world seem capable of savoring.

I feel my eyes beginning to drift shut, sinking into the first true peace I've tasted in what feels like a small eternity. Just when I teeter onto the precipice of blissful oblivion, I feel Louis shift minutely beside me.

"We're safe now, you know," he murmurs, so softly I barely catch the words. "Whatever had your hackles up back there."

One eye creaks open to find him studying me intently, those artfully tousled chestnut locks lending his casually immaculate appearance a roguish charm. His jade gaze is hypnotic in the dimness, somehow both resolute and infinitely inviting.

I search his expression, so invasive, yet equally incapable of even the slightest act of deception. It's there, in those unguarded windows to his soul, that I find my answer.

And more - a sense of security, of impregnable sanctuary that has been so scarce in the chaos of my life lately.

With a tremulous sigh, I let the last of the tension seep from my body and give in to the trust Louis has always, without question or falter, extended to me. Pillowing my head on his shoulder, I soak in the scents of cedar and home as the night whispers past outside our plush sanctuary.

"There was a man," I murmur, the truth slipping from my lips like water over a broken dam. "At the cafe, I thought I saw him...watching me."

Louis stills beside me, giving no outward reaction beyond the sudden stillness of a prize cat zeroing in on unseen prey. But I can sense it simmering beneath his composure - a vibration of fury and readiness that sends a chill trickling down my spine.

When he speaks again, his voice is a low, sibilant growl, rough from barely leashed restraint. "Did he approach you? Try anything?"

"No," I'm quick to reassure him, instinctively recoiling from the stark menace simmering behind those intense green eyes. "No, he...he just watched."

With painstaking slowness, I feel the tension begin to bleed from Louis's frame until he's once again radiating that aura of tranquil, almost preternatural composure.

"That's unacceptable," he mutters, more to himself than me. "I'll have it handled first thing tomorrow."

It's not a question or request, but a simple statement of fact from someone accustomed to determining his own reality rather than tolerating the ambitions of happenstance or interference.

There's a weight to the words, sheathed in velvety tones and delivered with the utmost casual politesse, but noticeable all the same. As if each precisely measured syllable is a tempered razor's edge capable of slicing straight through any obstacle.

With a shuddering breath, I burrow deeper into the shelter of his shoulder, chasing that oasis of warmth and safety. I don't ask what he means by "handled" or how far he intends to take matters into his own hands.

The truth is, some part of me simply doesn't care. That same instinctive corner that first tripped those panicked fight-or-flight signals has receded, quieted by the simple knowledge of Louis's undeniable resolve and the ferocious promise of protection that radiates from his very being.

Tomorrow can wait, along with all its turmoils and uncertainties.

Tonight, as the car whisks us away through the neon-drenched veins of the city, I am content to simply surrender to the one thing that has always felt steady and true amid the madness that has plagued my life.

Tonight, I am finally, blissfully, at peace.

The San Diego night wraps around me like a velvet glove, rich with the tang of the Pacific and the faintest whispers of revelry. I step out onto the terrace of the sleek Airbnb I've claimed as my temporary sanctuary, seeking solace in the warm coastal breezes.

From here, I can take in the glittering cityscape, all towering silhouettes and neon arteries pulsing with vibrant life. A neon sign beckoning to the thrill-seekers and pleasure-chasers, promising deliciously wicked delights under the shroud of night's murky embrace.

It should seduce me, this tantalizing invitation to indulge in the city's intoxicating heartbeat. But tonight, the allure feels muted, dimmed by an undercurrent of unease rippling through my veins like a premonition.

My fingers curl tighter around the railing as my gaze scans the deepening shadows beyond the pool of golden light haloing the terrace. Somewhere out there, predators lurk - their eyes glittering with ravenous hunger, scenting vulnerability on the warm night's breath.

Twisting a strand of hair between my fingers, I exhale slowly, savoring the salty caress of the evening breeze across my heated skin.

Breathe, just breathe.

Escape may prove elusive, but this fleeting illusion of tranquility is still mine to savor while it lasts. Because I know better than to trust in such fragile reprieves.

The other shoe always, inevitably, drops.

My grip tightens until the delicate bones in my hands ache in subconscious concert with the echoing ache pulsing between my thighs. Twin manifestations of the same profound yearning - to escape, yes, but also to surrender.

To revel in the very chaos from which I so desperately seek freedom.

Like gravity's cruel jest, the treacherous path of my thoughts leads inexorably back to June and the cataclysmic, almost supernaturally charged intensity that arcs between us. We are two star-crossed celestial bodies, fated to collide in an explosive, scorching conflagration that will surely consume us both.

My pulse races at the mere thought of his name, a white-hot spike of mingled lust and despair piercing straight through the armor I've tried so futilely to forge around my battered heart.

With a shuddering inhalation, I force myself to turn away from the terrace's threshold, retreating to the crisply appointed modernity of the rental's interior. The air-conditioned atmosphere within is a jarring transition from San Diego's balmy, tropical caress.

As the vapor-trailed scents of salt and seduction fade, I trail my fingers along the sofa's sleek contours, marveling at the impeccable minimalist aesthetic. Such pristine elegance, I find myself musing, my thoughts turning wry and scathing. How utterly transcendent it must feel to exist in this ephemeral temple of calculated serenity and good taste.

To be unshackled from the eternally messy, fraught burden of emotion and history. To simply be, unfettered by the bruising riptides of sentimentality and all its catastrophic undertow.

Is that what this place represents? An immaculate reliquary of thoughtful design and philosophies of mindful, purposeful living? Or is it merely a sterile monument to the detached, the perpetually vapid and hopelessly self-deluded?

The cynical twist of my lips mirrors the bitter line of my musings. But before I can untangle that particularly thorny thread of melancholia, a hushed thud and soft scrape of sound from the hallway beyond snaps my attention back into razor-sharp focus.

In a heartbeat, every nerve ending blazes with the crisp metallic tingle of adrenaline taking emergency precedence. Exhilaration and terror collide in a breathless standoff as I whirl toward the disturbance, body tensing in anticipation of fight-or-flight even before my lagging conscious mind has begun processing potential scenarios.

Then, like the detonation spark in a cataclysmic chain-reaction, his form melts from the pooling shadows of the hallway - an apparition rendered in equal shades of twilight and sin. Broad, powerful shoulders cleave through the darkness as an apex predator might emerge from its den, the city's reflected neon gilding the sharp, patrician lines of his jawline.

He coalesces from the gloom with an inexorable, irresistible gravity, like some profane Renaissance idol taking shape in candlelight. My mouth goes dry as my gaze rakes over the familiar topography of his features - from the high, severe slashes of those cheekbones to the piercing intensity that burns in depthless eyes.

June.

Just the wordless shape of his name on my lips sends a tremor of pure, visceral need lancing through me. A forbidden incantation to awaken the vortex of turbulent emotion and desire that perpetually roils between us, Charybdis to my hapless ship of state.

He moves with the coiled, leonine grace of a big cat, each footfall seeming to reverberate through the marrow of my bones until I can feel the bassy throb of it pulsing between my legs. His eyes, those viridian pools of merciless intensity, track over me with rapacious focus.

As if I were his prey, the object of some primal, insatiable need.

It's intoxicating and utterly terrifying, this sense of being something wild and hunted relegated under his simmering stare. A dizzying, exhilarating freefall into the promise of madness and reckless rapture, with only June's scorching ferocity to ensure my end is a glorious, all-consuming blaze.

He prowls the final span separating us without a single word, no veiled endearments or teasing quips. Just the rumbling current of predatory intent charged between us like a livewire, sizzling in the scant inches of space that now seem to have shrunk to a mere hairsbreadth.

Were it not for the subtle thrum of his respirations, I might have convinced myself this towering, feral creature was something indisputably supernatural bewitching me with its fae presence.

Up close, his austere beauty is nothing short of blinding. It steals the breath from my lungs, arrests every fleeting half-formed thought, until all that remains is the molten core of rapturous despair that binds me to this fatally dangerous man in ways I'm terrified to even try naming.

My hands reach for him in wordless, automatic instinct, fingers trembling as they encounter the twin delta grooves of his collar bones beneath the supple cotton of his shirt. Hard, uncompromising planes of muscle and sinew beneath that disquietingly affect a feral, undomesticated prowess I shouldn't find nearly as captivating as I do.

His lips quirk, the barest ghost of a smile slashing sharp and self-assured over aristocratic features. It's a look of infinite, indisputable possession and control - a gleaming obsidian dagger pressed against the dry, thundering pulse of my hammering heartbeat.

"Hello, Cara Mia." June's voice is liquid smoke and unholy psalms, equal parts benediction and damnation. "You're looking deliciously lost."

The words leave his lip, the way he looks at me—everything becomes crystal clear; And my knees buckle.

Juniper Deveaux has lost his fucking mind, and I deserve the padded cell right beside him...

Chapter 16
June

I step out of the shadows, a wraith given form, my entire being attuned to the siren's call of Cara's presence. The sight of her, a vision in the dim light of the Airbnb, sets my blood aflame with a hunger that borders on the profane.

"Hello, Cara Mia." The words slip from my tongue like a prayer and a curse, a dark invocation of the twisted devotion that consumes me. "You're looking deliciously lost."

Her eyes are a heady cocktail of fear and desire swirling in those fathomless depths. I prowl closer, each step deliberate, predatory, a wolf stalking its mate under the sway of a feral moon.

The sight of Cara, beautiful and vulnerable in the dim light, ignites a hunger in me that borders on madness. I close the distance between us with predatory intent, backing her against the wall until we are pressed together, heat to heat.

"You can't run from this forever, Cara," I growl, my voice rough with barely leashed need. "From what's between us. What's always been between us."

Her eyes are wide, luminous with mingled fear and longing. I can practically taste her inner war, the desperate battle between desire and self-preservation. It only makes me want her more.

Slowly, deliberately, I cage her in with my arms, my face hovering a mere whisper from hers. "I've missed you, Cara Mia. Craved you. You have no idea the depths of my obsession, how consuming it is."

"June..." She breathes my name like a plea and a warning, and the sound of it on her lips sends a bolt of pure, electric need straight to my core.

I close the distance between us, my body a hard, unyielding press against her softer curves. The scent of her, vanilla and spice and something uniquely Cara, fills my lungs, drowns my senses in a dizzying wave of want.

"You can't keep hiding from my love, Cara," I murmur, my lips grazing the delicate shell of her ear. "Sooner or later, you'll have to face the truth of what we are to each other."

She shudders in my hold, a full-body tremor that speaks of the war raging within her - the desperate yearning to surrender warring with the stubborn, prideful need to resist. I feel it in the tension of her muscles, the hitch in her breathing, the thundering of her pulse beneath my fingertips.

"And what truth is that, June?" She asks, defiance and need bleeding into her tone in equal measure. "That you're an obsessive, controlling bastard...who can't take I'm busy for an answer?"

I chuckle darkly, the sound rumbling through my chest and into hers. "Oh, Cara. We both know it's so much more than that." My hand comes up to cradle her jaw, tipping her face up to meet my burning gaze. "You're mine, just as I'm yours. Two halves of the same twisted, fucked-up whole."

The truth of it hangs heavy in the air between us, a palpable force that seems to crackle and hum like a live wire. I can see it in her eyes, the reluctant acknowledgment, the bone-deep recognition of the inescapable bond that tethers her soul to mine.

"I won't let you go," I vow, my thumb stroking over the plush swell of her bottom lip. "I can't. Not when every fiber of my being screams out for you, aches to possess you, to consume you until there's nothing left but the ecstasy of our union."

Cara's breath hitches, her lips parting beneath my touch as if begging to be claimed. I lean in, a hair's breadth separating our mouths, the anticipation a sweet, excruciating agony. "Let me in, Cara Mia," I coax, my voice a rough, honeyed growl. "Surrender to me, to us, and I'll show you pleasures you've never even dreamed of."

For a moment, the world seems to hold its breath, suspended on the knife's edge of her decision. I can feel the war within her, the push and pull of longing and fear, need and self-preservation. And then, like a dam finally crumbling under the relentless onslaught of the tide, she breaks.

Her mouth crashes against mine, a fierce, desperate claiming that steals the air from my lungs and sets my blood to boiling. I respond with equal fervor, my hands gripping her hips, yanking her flush against me until there's no space left between us, no room for doubt or hesitation.

We move together in a frantic dance of lips and teeth and tongue, a primal give and take as old as time itself. Clothes are torn away with reckless abandon, buttons scattering like fallen stars across the hardwood floor. Skin meets skin in a blaze of heat and friction, every touch a searing brand, every caress a wordless vow.

I hoist her up, her legs wrapping around my waist as I carry her to the bedroom, our mouths never breaking contact. We tumble onto the bed in a tangle of limbs, the cool silk of the sheets a shocking contrast to the inferno raging between us.

"Say you're mine," I command, my hand skimming down the quivering plane of her stomach to delve into the slick, molten heat at her core. "Say it, Cara. Let me hear you."

She arches into my touch, a broken moan falling from her lips as I stroke her most sensitive flesh with ruthless precision. "I'm yours," she gasps out, her nails raking down my back hard enough to draw blood. "God help me, June, I'm yours."

Those words, that sweet, hard-won surrender, unleash something feral and untamed within me. I set about worshiping her body with a single-minded intensity, determined to wring every last drop of pleasure from her until she's boneless and spent beneath me.

A dark chuckle rumbles in my chest as I trace the delicate line of her jaw. "Don't you see? Nothing about us has ever been right. But it's real. Visceral. Inevitable."

My lips find her neck, worshiping the frantic flutter of her pulse. Cara arches into me, a broken whimper escaping her throat. The sound is my undoing.

I drink in the sight of her—all tousled hair and kiss-swollen lips, a debauched goddess in the making. I stroke and tease her like a maestro playing his instrument. She writhes beneath my ministrations, teetering on the knife's edge of ecstasy.

"Let go for me, Cara," I command, my voice strained with need as I hold her tightly against the wall.

Her body trembles in my grasp, but she fights against it, her feral pride evident in every tilt of her chin and clench of her fists.

I know I must earn her surrender, prove myself worthy of possessing her completely.

So I drop to my knees, kissing and caressing her body until she writhes beneath me.

With every moan and gasp, I feel her control slipping away. And when she finally shatters around me, her thighs quake around my ears.

"June!" Cara screams my name loudly.

Only then do I allow myself release—without her touch, or the pleasure of her wet cunt—spilling hotly on my own skin. I know Cara owns me.

"There's no escape now," I murmur into her hair, holding her tight as we both catch our breath. "You've always been mine, Cara. And you'll never break free of me."

As she relaxes in my embrace, I revel in the full weight of my obsession for her. She is everything to me, and I would burn the world down before ever releasing her.

As the aftershocks slowly subside, I roll to the side, gathering her boneless form into the shelter of my arms. She burrows into my chest, her ear pressed to the thundering cadence of my heart, and I feel a fierce swell of possessiveness, of protectiveness, rise up within me.

"Stay with me," I murmur into the silken cloud of her hair, my fingers tracing idle patterns along the dip of her spine. "Stay, and let me love you the way you deserve to be loved."

She's silent for a long moment, and I feel a flicker of unease, of fear that she'll retreat back behind her walls, that she'll deny the undeniable pull between us. But then she tilts her head up, her eyes meeting mine, and the tenderness, the raw vulnerability I see there steals the breath from my lungs.

"Okay," she whispers, her fingers coming up to trace the line of my jaw, the curve of my lip. "I'll stay. God help me, June, but I'll stay."

And with those words, the broken pieces of my world finally slot back into place. She is mine, and I am hers, and nothing - not my family, not her fears, not the demons that haunt us both - will ever tear us apart again.

Because in the end, this is what we were always meant to be. Two shattered souls finding completion, absolution, in the arms of the only person who could ever truly understand the darkness within.

And as I crush her to me, sealing our pact with a kiss that feels like a promise and a prayer, I know that I will burn the world to ash before I ever let her go again.

Cara Mia, mi amor, my salvation and my damnation - she is the beginning and the end of me, the axis upon which my entire universe turns.

And I will fight for her, bleed for her, die for her if that's what it takes to keep her by my side, now and forever.

Because in the end, that's the only truth that matters. She is mine, and I am hers, and together, we will stand against the world and all its petty cruelties.

A love like ours, fierce and primal and all-consuming - it's the stuff of legends, of myths and fairy tales.

And I will be damned if I let anyone or anything stand in the way of our happily ever after.

As the night wraps around us, I let myself sink into the warmth of her body, the steady rise and fall of her breathing a soothing metronome against my chest.

And for the first time in longer than I can remember, I feel something that might almost be mistaken for peace settling into the fractured crevices of my soul.

Because she is here, in my arms, where she was always meant to be; what it means to be truly, madly, irrevocably in love.

For I am lost, willingly and completely, in the obsession of her.

I jolt awake, heart pounding and skin slick with sweat. Instinctively, I reach for Cara, craving the reassurance of her warmth, but my fingers grasp only cold, empty sheets. Panic slices through me like a blade, and I bolt upright, eyes frantically scanning the room.

No. No, no, no. She can't be gone. Not after everything we shared, the promises whispered in the dark.

But the signs of her absence are undeniable. Her clothes, haphazardly discarded in the heat of our passion, are nowhere to be seen. The air is stale, devoid of her intoxicating scent. The only trace of her presence is the lingering indent on the pillow beside me.

A bitter laugh escapes my lips, as the reality of my actions crashes over me.

What the fuck was I thinking? Ambushing Cara like that, following her to San Diego, into her bed, - I had no right.This isn't the casual, no-strings arrangement she requested - I can never be just some faceless fuck buddy to her.

No, I want it all. I crave my sweet Cara Mia beneath me, quaking with pleasure night after night, for the rest of my wretched days.

The plan takes shape, twisted and intricate. I'll prove myself worthy, show the depths of my devotion. I'll become the man she deserves, then sweep her off her feet, reclaim her as my own once more.

It's a deranged, delusional scheme - I know that, deep down. But the alternative, living without Cara...that's a fate worse than eternal torment. I can't let her go.

God damn my wretched soul for all eternity, but I'll have her. I'll make Cara Mia mine, my wife, before she even realizes what's happened.

Stumbling out of bed, I pace the room like a caged animal, my mind spinning with regret and recrimination. I have to find her. I need to fix this, fix us.

But before I can execute my plan, the phone trills, breaking the oppressive silence. Judith's name flashes on the screen, and my stomach drops.

Shit.

The memory of our last conversation, of the hurt and disappointment in her voice, twists like a knife in my gut. Bracing myself, I answer, my voice rough with unshed emotion. "Jude, I—"

"Save it, June," she cuts me off, her tone sharper than I've ever heard it. "I don't want to hear any more excuses or empty promises."

I flinch, each word a lash against my fractured psyche. "I'm sorry," I rasp out, the inadequacy of the apology bitter on my tongue. "God, Jude, I'm so fucking sorry."

"You should be," she snaps, fury and hurt bleeding through the static. "Do you have any idea the mess you've left in your wake?"

I close my eyes, forcing down the lump in my throat. "Jude, I... I'm sorry. For everything. I've been so lost, so caught up in my own bullshit, and I've hurt you in the process."

A long pause, punctuated by a weary sigh. "Yeah, you have. But that's not the only reason I'm pissed, June. Mom's on a warpath. Apparently, you said something to Amethyst that has her in tears. What the hell were you thinking?"

Shame crashes over me in nauseating waves as the memory of my cruelty, my unhinged cruelty, plays in vivid technicolor. The vicious words I spewed, the utter lack of control or compassion. I squeeze my eyes shut, bile rising in my throat.

"I'll fix it," I manage, the words sticking in my throat. "I'll make things right, Jude, I swear. With you, with Mom, with Amethyst. I just... I need to find Cara first."

"No, June," Judith cuts in, her voice brooking no argument. "What you need is to get your shit together and stop running after a woman who clearly wants nothing to do with you."

The harsh truth of her words feels like a sucker-punch to the gut, stealing the breath from my lungs. Because she's right. My relentless pursuit of Cara, my inability to respect her wishes, her boundaries, is the root of this whole twisted mess.

"You're right," I admit, the confession scraping my throat raw. "I've been selfish, obsessive, toxic. But Jude... I love her. So fucking much. And I don't know how to stop."

There's a long pause, heavy with unspoken emotion. When Judith speaks again, her voice is softer, laced with an aching mix of sympathy and resignation. "I know, Junie. But your love... it's poisoned right now. It's consuming you, making you someone neither of us recognizes."

Tears burn my eyes, blurring the room into a haze of muted colors. "I don't know how to fix it," I confess, my voice breaking. "How to be the man she deserves, the brother you need me to be."

There's a long, weighted silence, and I can practically hear the gears turning in Judith's mind. "I want to believe you, June. I really do. But you've got a long road ahead of you, and it starts with getting your shit together and respecting Cara's choices, even if they don't involve you."

I nod, forgetting for a moment that she can't see me. "I will," I promise, the words heavy with resolve. "I'll do whatever it takes, Jude. I just... I need you to know how sorry I am. For everything."

She sighs, and I can picture her running a hand through her chestnut waves, a habit she's had since childhood. "I'm here for you, Junie. Always. But you've got to do the work. And that starts with a sincere apology to Amethyst and some serious groveling to get back in Mom's good graces."

The thought of facing Amethyst, of owning up to my cruelty, fills me with dread. But it's a small price to pay for the chance to start making things right.

"Okay," I agree, my voice rough with emotion. "I'll talk to Amethyst, and I'll deal with Mom. But Jude... thank you. For not giving up on me, even when I've given you every reason to."

"That's what family does, little brother. We fight, we fuck up, but we don't bail. Now go clean up your messes. And June?"

"Yeah?"

"When you find Cara, and I know you will... be honest with her. Lay yourself bare, even if it's terrifying...or don't contact her at all."

With that, she's gone, the click of the line echoing like a shot in the sudden stillness. I stare at the phone, my resolve hardening into something solid and immovable.

But first, it's time to face the music and fury of my mother.

Chapter 17
Cara

I'm plummeting. Rudely shoved and recklessly free falling as the dreamscape dissolves, and the visceral sensation of being forcibly dropped back into my own body sets every nerve on edge.

My heart thunders against my ribcage, a caged hummingbird desperate for escape. Conspiracy and confusion twist through me like a treacherous vine, made worse by the shadows dancing across the unfamiliar walls in a sinister ballet.

This strange, unsettling landscape brings my paranoia alive, every creak and groan stoking my mounting anxiety.

It takes a moment for the events of the previous night to come flooding back - June's sudden appearance, our mini fuck fest, the desperate promises whispered in the dark.

Turning, I expect to find him beside me, but the bed is empty. Panic grips my throat, until I make out his silhouette by the window, silver moonlight painting his chiseled features with heavenly highlights.

"June?" My voice breaks from fitful sleep, barely a whisper, but he hears me anyway.

"Sorry, did I wake you?" He moves back to the bed, perching on the edge, his hand finding mine atop the sheets. His skin is cool, as if he's been standing by that open window for hours, lost in thought.

I shake my head. "What time is it?"

"Just past 3 AM," he murmurs. "You looked so peaceful, and I didn't want to leave without telling you goodbye."

But something in his tone, a distant quality, sets off alarm bells in my head. I sit up, pulling the sheet with me, studying his face in the dimness. "June, why were you here? In San Diego, at my rental?"

He's silent for a long moment, and I can practically hear the cogs turning in his head, choosing his words carefully. "I needed to see you, Cara. I couldn't bear the thought of you here, with..." He trails off, but I can fill in the blanks.

With Louis. With anyone else.

Suspicion sinks its claws into my chest, squeezing the air from my lungs. Was he the one stalking me? Following my every move like some twisted guardian angel?

The thought makes my stomach churn, bile rising in my throat. No, I try to reassure myself. June would never do that. He's intense, possessive even, but he wouldn't cross that line.

Would he?

June must sense my growing unease, because he suddenly pulls me into his arms, enveloping me in a tight embrace. "Cara, I'm so sorry. I know I shouldn't have come, but I...I miss you."

His voice is strained, raw with emotion, and something in the way he holds me makes me pause, the sharp edges of my suspicion softening ever so slightly.

"How did you find me, June?" I ask, the words muffled against his chest.

He sits up, running a hand through his tousled hair. "Can't I just miss my Cara Mia?" His thumb strokes my hand gently. "And, you just texted me some vague response about being busy. I couldn't bear the thought of being apart any longer."

I shake my head, frustration bubbling up inside me. "That's not what I asked. How did you know where I was staying?"

He exhales, the sound shaky and vulnerable in the still room. "I'm a Deveaux, Cara. I have resources, connections. It wasn't difficult for me to find out where you were."

June pauses, his thumb continuing its soothing motions. "But I didn't come here to scare you or force anything. I just... I couldn't stay away from you."

His words, meant to reassure, only fuel the growing sense of unease in my stomach.

Resources.

Connections.

The implications make my skin crawl. Has he been having me followed? Watched? The thought is almost too much to bear.

I try to slip out of his arms; failing horribly, the sheets tangling around my legs like grasping hands. June also refusing to let go, his arms flex as he locks me in.

And panic seizes me in a nauseating grip.

"I'll be right back," I whisper, proud of how steady my voice sounds despite the tremor in my bones. "I'm just going to pee."

"No, you can use my mouth as a toilet." He moans, biting my ear as he continues. "Your thighs will keep my ears warm."

"God alone knows, what kind of things you rich people are into," I joke lamely. "But that's not my kink. I'll be back."

I don't wait for a response, practically sprinting to the bathroom, the door slamming shut behind me with a finality that does little to calm the rioting of my pulse. With shaking fingers, I fumble for my phone, tears blurring the screen as I type out a frantic message to Louis.

Emergency. Need to go home. Can you bring my stuff later? So sorry.

I hit send and sink to the cold tile floor, drawing my knees up to my chest as if I can physically hold myself together. The phone vibrates almost immediately, Louis' concerned reply glowing in the dimness.

Of course. You okay? Need me there now?

I hesitate, my thumbs hovering over the keys. Louis has been my rock, my safe harbor in the storm. But this is a tempest I need to weather on my own.

I'm okay. Just need to get to family. Talk soon. And thank you.

Wiping angrily at the tears streaking down my cheeks, I force myself to stand on shaky legs. The four walls of this rental suddenly feel like a cage, closing in around me, and I can't bear the thought of seeing June again.

The letters, the constant unease - it all makes a sickening kind of sense now. The urge to scream, to shatter the mirror and watch the shards rain down like glittering tears, is almost overwhelming.

But I can't break, not now, not here. I have to get out, have to put distance between me and the man who may not be who I thought he was. The man I've loved with every fractured piece of my heart.

I splash cold water on my face, the shock of it grounding me in the present. Squaring my shoulders, I open the door, steeling myself for what waits on the other side.

Panic grips me again, a nauseating wave of fear and disorientation. I feel like I'm going crazy. I can't stay here, I have to get out, get somewhere safe.

Carefully, I open the bathroom door, peering out into the bedroom. June is sprawled face-down on the bed, unmoving. I hold my breath, watching for any sign that he's aware of my movements.

Satisfied that he's oblivious, I quietly slip out of the bathroom, tiptoeing towards the door. My gaze falls on the side table, where my purse sits. Without a second thought, I snatch it up, the weight of it in my hand a small comfort.

As I reach for the doorknob, a floorboard creaks beneath my feet, and I freeze, my heart pounding. June stirs, letting out a muffled groan, and I hold my breath, praying he doesn't wake.

After what feels like an eternity, he settles back into stillness, and I seize the opportunity, slipping out the door and closing it silently behind me. With a shaky exhale, I hurry down the stairs and out into the cool night air, scanning the street for the waiting car.

There, just a short distance away, I spot the Uber, and I practically sprint to it, throwing myself into the passenger seat.

"Go, go, go," I plead, my voice trembling.

The driver nods, pulling away from the curb as I sink into the worn leather seat, my heart still racing. I'm out, I'm safe, but the weight of what's happened, of June's betrayal, threatens to crush me.

Tears spill down my cheeks as the city lights blur past, and I wrap my arms around myself, trying to hold the pieces of my shattered composure together. I feel so alone, so violated in the one place I should have felt secure.

But I can't go back, I won't. The thought of facing June again, of having to confront the truth of his actions, is more than I can bear right now.

The rumble of the plane's engines reverberates through the cabin, a steady pulse that does little to calm the chaos of my life. I take a deep, steadying breath, but it fails to soothe the turmoil coursing through me.

Glancing out the window, I watch the city lights shrink into the distance, a physical representation of the emotional gulf that now separates us. Part of me longs to look back, to see if June is standing there, watching as I flee.

But I resist the urge, to want him...to indulge in a sick fantasy that someone could love me this much and still be sane—or even, good for me. I have to let go, to move on, even if every fiber of my being aches to turn back.

So I'll go forward, grow through this pain and go where I know I'll be safe.

Safe where my family is, where my longtime refuge awaits - the thought of returning there, of immersing myself in the familiar comfort of home, is the only thing keeping me grounded in this moment.

Home to Accel City.

Thr bustling metropolis that's been my playground with June, beckons in the distance, its towering skyscrapers a beacon of hope in the inky night.

As the plane climbs higher, the turbulence jostling my nerves, I can feel the adrenaline slowly ebbing from my system.

Exhaustion seeps into my bones, the weight of the day's events finally catching up to me. I sink deeper into the seat, grateful for the relative solitude of my window row.

My mind races, replaying every moment, every detail of June's reappearance. The cool distance in his voice, the careful way he chose his words - it all speaks to a level of premeditation that chills me to the core.

He knew where I was, how to find me. The implications are enough to send a fresh wave of nausea rolling through my stomach.

How long has he been following me?

Is he behind the letters, the black cars trailing me...but why would he warn me away to follow me around like some exotic animal in his free range zoo.

The thought makes my skin crawl, it feels like a violation, and I can't seem to shake the idea that he was behind the scenes pulling the strings of my life...like I was his twisted little contortionist.

To use a prey, just to bend and break me at his will.

I wrap my arms around myself, as if I can physically hold the pieces of my shattered sense of security together.

June is my best friend...or was he just obsessed with me. Poor little Cara.

First generation American borne to an illegal Italian girl desperate for shelter, and the good Nigerian doctor who married her for the money.

Will I ever feel safe again?

The question lingers, a heavy, ominous weight that threatens to drag me under. I squeeze my eyes shut, willing the tears that threaten to fall to hold back just a little while longer.

I need space, air... I need my sister.

The moment I step through the door, a sob tears through my body, ripping away the last shreds of my composure.

"Sonya!" I cry out, my voice raw and desperate, echoing through the house like a wounded animal. "Sonya, where are you?"

But it's not my baby sister's face that appears in the doorway. It's Mama, her eyes wide with alarm, her hands already outstretched to catch me as I crumble.

"Cara, baby, what's wrong?" she asks, her voice laced with worry as she pulls me into her arms. But I can't answer, can't find the words to express the chaos that's raging inside me.

All I can do is cling to her, my tears soaking into the soft fabric of her robe, my body shaking with the force of my sobs.

She murmurs soothing words, her fingers carding through my tangled hair, but I barely hear her over the roar of my own thoughts.

June's face flashes through my mind, his eyes dark with a possession that now feels more like a threat than a promise. The doubts and fears that have been festering in the back of my mind come rushing to the surface, spilling from my lips in a torrent of anguished words.

Mama guides me to the couch, her hands never leaving my shoulders, but this time her presence isn't enough. I need my mini me, and the only best friend I'll ever need.

And then Sonya is there, appearing as if summoned by the force of my distress.

"Who do I need to kill?" she asks, only half-joking.

I shake my head, unable to find the words, but Sonya doesn't need them. Song and Sonya may be twins that share a brain; but my mini me and I—we share a heart.

One look at my tear-stained face—at the way I'm clinging to Mama latched like a newborn at the tit—her expression hardens, death's grim scythe gleaming in her eyes.

Sonya knows, just as surely as I do, that something has gone terribly, terribly wrong.

"What did he do?" she demands, her voice low and dangerous. "What did that bastard do to you?"

She sinks onto the couch beside me, pulling me into her arms, and I let myself fall apart, the sobs tearing through me like a hurricane.

Sonya holds me tightly, her own tears mingling with mine, her anger a palpable force in the air around us.

"I'll kill him," she whispers, her voice trembling with rage. "I swear to God, Cara, if he hurt you, I'll fucking kill him."

But even as the words leave her lips, I know it's not that simple. Because even now, even with the fear and the doubt coursing through my veins, I can't deny the truth that's written on my heart.

I love him. God help me, I love him still.

And that's what makes this so much worse, so much harder to bear. Because if June, the man who holds my heart in his hands, is capable of this kind of betrayal, then what does that say about me? What does it say about the love I thought we shared?

I cling to Sonya, to Mama, as if they're the only thing keeping me tethered to the world. And in a way, they are. They're my anchor, my safe harbor, the only constants in a life that feels like it's spinning out of control.

We sit like that for a long time, a tangle of limbs and shared heartache, as the sky brightens around us. Sonya whispers filled with promises of protection, of retribution, while Mama murmurs soft words of comfort, of understanding.

And slowly, gradually, I feel the panic begin to recede, the tightness in my chest easing ever so slightly. I know this is only the beginning, that there are hard conversations and painful decisions ahead.

But for now, in the warmth and love of my sister's embrace, I allow myself to believe that maybe, just maybe, I can find my way through this darkness.

That maybe, even with a shattered heart and a broken trust, there is still hope for tomorrow.

The night passes in a haze of tears and whispered reassurances, Mama and Sonya's presence a constant comfort. As dawn breaks, painting the sky in soft hues of pink and orange, I finally succumb to exhaustion, falling into a fitful slumber on the couch.

When I wake, the sun is high in the sky, streaming through the windows in warm, honey-colored rays. For a moment, I'm disoriented, the events of the previous night feeling like a distant nightmare. But then it all comes rushing back, and I sit up with a gasp, my heart pounding in my chest.

The sound of voices from the kitchen draws my attention, and I pad softly across the hardwood floors, following the scent of freshly brewed coffee and something sweet baking in the oven.

As I round the corner, I freeze, taking in the scene before me. Song and Louis are seated at the kitchen table, their heads bent close together as they speak in low, urgent tones. Sonya is at the stove, flipping pancakes with a determined focus, while Mama bustles around, setting out plates and mugs.

"What's going on?" I ask, my voice rough from sleep and tears.

Four pairs of eyes snap to me, a mixture of concern and relief on their faces. Song is out of his seat in an instant, crossing the room to pull me into a tight hug.

"Cara, thank God you're awake. We were so worried about you."

I melt into his embrace, breathing in the familiar scent of his cologne. "I'm sorry," I mumble into his shoulder. "I didn't mean to scare you all."

Louis appears at my side, his hand resting on the small of my back in a gesture of comfort. "You have nothing to apologize for, Cara. We're just glad you're safe."

Mama ushers us all to the table, insisting that I eat something before we dive into the heavy topics that loom over us like storm clouds. I pick at my pancakes, my stomach too knotted with anxiety to have much of an appetite.

Finally, when the silence becomes too heavy to bear, I set down my fork and look around at the faces of my loved ones. "I suppose you're all wondering what happened last night."

Sonya reaches across the table, taking my hand in hers. "Only if you're ready to talk about it, sis. We're here to listen, not to pry."

I take a deep breath, steeling myself for the words that need to be said. "June showed up at my rental in San Diego. In the middle of the night. He said he needed to see me, that he couldn't stay away."

Mama's brow furrows, concern etching deep lines into her face. "But how did he know where you were staying?"

I shake my head, frustration and fear warring in my chest. "That's just it. I don't know. He said he has resources, connections. That it wasn't hard for him to find me."

Song's jaw clenches, his eyes hardening. "That's not okay, Cara. That's stalking, plain and simple."

Louis nods, his expression grim. "Song's right. No matter how he tries to spin it, what June did was a violation of your privacy and your trust."

I feel tears prickling at the corners of my eyes, the validation of my fears both a relief and a crushing blow. "I just don't know what to think," I whisper, my voice cracking. "I love him, but... how can I trust him after this?"

Mama reaches across the table, taking my other hand in her weathered grasp. "Oh, honey. I wish I had all the answers. But what I do know is that you are strong, and brave, and capable of making the right choice for yourself. And no matter what you decide, we will be here to support you every step of the way."

Sonya nods, fierce determination blazing in her eyes. "Damn right, we will. You're not alone in this, Cara. Not now, not ever."

As I look around at the faces of my family, at the love and loyalty shining in their eyes, I feel a flicker of hope spark to life in my chest. Maybe, just maybe, I can find my way through this darkness. Maybe, with their help, I can come out the other side stronger than before.

But there's one more piece of news that needs to be shared, one bright spot amidst the turmoil. I turn to Song and Louis, a small smile tugging at the corners of my lips.

"So, while we're all here, is there anything else you two want to tell us?"

Song's eyes widen, a blush creeping up his neck as he glances at Louis. "Well, actually... Louis and I, we're..."

"Together," Louis finishes, taking Song's hand in his own. "Romantically. It's new, but it's real."

For a moment, the kitchen is silent, the weight of their revelation hanging in the air. Then Sonya is out of her seat, a squeal of delight erupting from her lips as she throws her arms around them both.

"I knew it! I fucking knew it! This is the best news ever!"

Mama's reaction is more subdued, but no less joyful. She rises from her chair, cupping their faces in her hands and pressing a tender kiss to each of their foreheads.

"Love is a precious gift," she murmurs, her eyes shining with unshed tears. "Cherish it, nurture it. Don't let it slip away."

As I watch the scene unfold, a bittersweet mix of happiness and longing swirls in my chest. To see a love story blossoming, pure and untainted by the shadows of doubt... it's a poignant reminder of everything I once had with June. Everything I fear may now be lost.

But I refuse to let my own pain dim the light of their joy. They deserve this moment, this celebration of their love. And I will be damned if I let my broken heart steal that from them.

So I rise from my seat, crossing the room to pull them both into a fierce hug. "I'm so happy for you," I whisper, meaning every word. "You two are perfect for each other. Don't let anyone tell you different."

As the morning unfolds, filled with laughter and tears, shared stories and gentle reassurances, I feel the weight on my chest begin to ease. The road ahead is still shrouded in uncertainty, the path unclear and fraught with pain.

But here, in the warmth and love of my family, I know I am not alone. Together, we will weather this storm. Together, we will find a way through the darkness.

And maybe, just maybe, I will emerge on the other side stronger, wiser, and ready to face whatever the future may hold.

Even if that future doesn't include June Deveaux.

Chapter 18
June

Fuck. Fuckity fucking fuck. The silence of my penthouse is deafening, broken only by the incessant ticking of the antique clock on the mantelpiece. Each second feels like a goddamn eternity as I pace back and forth, Cara's absence a palpable ache in my chest. My phone, clutched tightly in my hand, remains stubbornly silent, mocking me with its lack of notifications.

It's been days since I last saw her, since I last heard her voice. Days of pure, unadulterated hell. Every unanswered call, every ignored text, is a twist of the knife in my gut. I can't bear the thought of losing her, of letting my fucking mistakes and my twisted obsession drive her away forever.

I've tried everything, like a pathetic lovesick puppy. Showing up at her house, planting flowers in her garden as a silent apology, a permanent reminder of my love. But even as I dig my hands into the rich soil, I know it's not enough. It will never be enough, not until I grow a pair and face the ugly truth of what I've done, lay myself bare before her.

But first, I gotta handle this clusterfuck of a situation at the office. Pops' legacy is crumbling, and it's on me to save it. Me, the prodigal son, the black sheep. Fucking ironic, isn't it?

My phone buzzes, Judith's name flashing on the screen. I hesitate, my thumb hovering over the answer button.

But I can't deal with her right now, can't handle her well-meaning concern and pressing demands. I let it go to voicemail, shoving the device back into my pocket with a curse.

I need to clear my head, to escape this suffocating penthouse and the ghosts of my own making. I grab my keys, stomping towards the door with single-minded determination. My nerves are a mess by the time I get to Cara's family duplex.

But before I can ring the bell, the door opens, and I'm greeted by a sight that stops me dead in my tracks.

"Juniper Deveaux." Cara's mom stands before me, her eyes hard and cold, her lips pressed into a thin line of disapproval. "It's not a pleasure today, I'm afraid."

Fuck me sideways. This is the last thing I need right now. I open my mouth to speak, to plead my case, but she cuts me off with a sharp gesture.

"I don't know whether to strangle you with that fancy belt or put you over my knee and discipline you with it," she hisses, her words dripping with venom. "I've always liked you, blamed your lack of manners and commitment issues on your faulty parents. But today, your mother has the audacity to bring herself to my door, to come into my home just to insult my child and my motherhood, trying to buy your freedom. And now, after what I've learned, you have the gumption to step foot on my doormat and ask to see my child?"

She takes a step closer, her finger jabbing into my chest, and I feel my stomach drop. "*Vai a cagare*! And if I find out you were the one stalking her, sending her letters and threats, messing with the chance for me to have grandbabies, well, I ought to..."

She trails off, her chest heaving with barely contained rage, and I feel the full weight of my actions crashing down on me. I've not only betrayed Cara, but I've brought pain and suffering to her entire family.

"I'm sorry," I manage to choke out, my voice rough and strained. "I never meant to hurt her, to hurt any of you. I just... I love her so fucking much, and I got lost in that love, in my fear of losing her."

Cara's mother shakes her head, unmoved by my pathetic attempt at an apology. "That's not love, June. That's possession, obsession. And it has no place in my daughter's life. Now go, before I do something we'll both regret."

With a final, piercing glare, she slams the door in my face, leaving me standing in the hallway like a fucking idiot. I lean my forehead against the cool wood, my heart shattering into a million jagged pieces. She's right, I know she is. I've crossed a line that can never be uncrossed. But the thought of losing Cara, of never again basking in the warmth of her presence, is a fate worse than death.

I trudge back to my car, my feet heavy as lead. The drive to the office passes in a blur, my mind lost in a haze of self-loathing and despair. I ignore the curious glances from my employees, storming past them like a man possessed.

As I round the corner to my office, I catch sight of a familiar figure. Alex. What the fuck are they doing here? And then, they see me...

"Don't get your designer panties all twisted, Deveaux," Alex grins. "I just came for lunch with a friend. Or can't I hang with our other friends."

I stride up to them, getting too far up in their grill, but I can't find fucks left to give. "Cara? Is she your lunch date?"

"You've gotten so fucking weird man, and it's not in a good way. Dude, you're obsessed as shit." Alex rolls their eyes, pushing me back a step. "Maybe you should get to the nearest shrink!" With that, they turn heel and leave.

The rejection smarted for sure, but a niggling suspicion remains. I pace back to my office, tempted to punch straight through the frosted glass door.

My head throbs, some Poe-level thumping threatening to crack my skull wide open. How the fuck did things spiral so spectacularly?

Answer's crystal clear when I think on it - I'm a jealous fool who doesn't deserve the goddess I worship. The sickest part? I legit don't know if I can stop chasing her.

Cara's the elixir in my veins, the fucking oxygen in my lungs. Losing her would be beyond catastrophic...it'd be damn apocalyptic.

Fuck me sideways. I barely make it two steps into the office before I'm ambushed by a wall of muscle in cheap suits. Mother's goons, no doubt.

"Mr. Deveaux," the beefiest of the lot grunts, "your mother requests your presence at the mansion. Immediately."

I bark out a laugh, harsh and humorless. "Oh, she 'requests' it, does she? Well, you can kindly inform Mother Dearest that I have no intention of playing her twisted little games today. I've got bigger fucking fish to fry."

I try to shoulder past them, but they're unmovable, a human barricade blocking my path. Rage simmers under my skin, white-hot and ready to blow.

"I ain't asking," Beefy sneers. "You're coming with us, whether you like it or not."

Oh, hell no. No one tells Juniper fucking Deveaux what to do, not even on my mother's orders. I straighten to my full height, channeling every ounce of icy authority I possess.

"Listen carefully, because I despise repeating myself. I am not going anywhere with you meatheads. I have urgent business to attend to, business that does not involve indulging my mother's megalomaniacal power trips. So kindly fuck off before I make you regret ever setting foot in my office."

For a moment, they look uncertain, thrown off balance by the steel in my voice. I seize the opportunity, dodging around them with surprising agility and making a break for the elevator.

"Hey!" Beefy shouts, but I'm already gone, smashing the 'close door' button with vindictive glee.

As the elevator descends, I lean against the wall, my heart jackhammering against my ribs. Fuck, that was close. Too close. Mother's little ambush only confirms my worst suspicions - she's up to something, something big and bad and designed to royally screw me over.

Well, not today, Satan. Not fucking today.

I need to regroup, to figure out my next move. And I need to find Cara, to explain everything and beg for her forgiveness, even if I have to camp outside her window with a goddamn boombox like some cliché rom-com hero.

But first, I need to go home and change. Can't grovel in style without my lucky 'I'm a fuckup, please forgive me' tie, can I?

I peel out of the parking garage like a bat out of hell, weaving through midday traffic with reckless abandon. Every second counts, every moment drawing me closer to the inevitable confrontation with the dual forces of my mother's tyranny and Cara's justified wrath.

My tires screech to a halt outside my building, tossing the keys to the valet and storming inside. The elevator ride to the penthouse feels interminable, my skin itching with impatience and dread.

I'm shouldering through my front door, ready to grab my shit and go...the universe must fucking despise me 'cause I get cock-blocked hard at my own front door, my blood running cold at the sight that greets me.

And then, I hear it - a lilting voice that sends ripples of dread down my spine. "Oh Juniper, darling, you're finally home!"

Mother. Here. Now. Fuck me gently with a chainsaw.

I storm towards the ungodly sight that greets me, biting back a stream of curses...

A full-fledged OBGYN setup invades my living room, complete with stirrups and ultrasound machine. Amethyst and Doc Volkner flank it, expressions carved from infuriatingly smug granite.

"What in the ever-loving fuck is this?" I growl, glaring daggers at my mother.

She titters, a Stepford Chucky doll nightmare come to life. "Why, it's the next step in your legacy, sweetheart. Amethyst here has so generously offered her womb to propagate our line. Even after you insulted her; Isn't it marvelous? And to ensure optimal results, the good doctor shall oversee the fertilization process from start to finish."

Bile scorches my throat, stomach heaving at the batshit insanity unfolding. "Absofuckinglutely NOT. Cease and desist this madness right fucking now. I will never, and I mean NEVER, be party to this...this clusterfuck!"

Mother's eyes flash, polite facade cleaved away to reveal the soulless harpy lurking underneath. Her talons emerge as she points one deadly-sharp finger at me, voice dropping into the sub-zero range.

"You WILL do this, Juniper. You WILL perform your duty as a Deveaux heir. After all, it's not like you have a choice, now, is it?"

At her nod, six hulking meatheads in black suits emerge from the shadows to flank the exit, a impenetrable wall of flesh and muscle blocking my escape.

The message is painfully clear - comply or else. And in that moment, staring down the barrel of my mother's twisted machinations, I wonder if I've finally met the one foe I cannot outmaneuver.

Judith's warning echoes in my skull: without an heir, the entire Deveaux empire would crumble to ashes. Do I let it all burn for love, or do I sacrifice my very soul on the pyre of familial obligation?

Mother's voice drips with false sweetness, a saccharine venom that sets my teeth on edge. "It's time you retired chasing after that little tart, and come to your senses Juniper Deveaux."

Red. All I see is fucking red. How dare she...

"You watch your forked tongue," I snarl, stalking forward until we're practically nose to nose. "You don't get to talk about Cara, not now, not ever."

Mother's lips curve into a smile, sharp and ruthless. "Touched a nerve, did I? How terribly inconsiderate of me. But really, darling, it's time to put aside this foolish infatuation and focus on what truly matters - your duty to this family."

She gestures grandly to the unholy medical nightmare that has taken over my home. "Amethyst has generously agreed to bear the next Deveaux heir. Dr. Volkner here will oversee the conception and ensure everything goes smoothly. Isn't it marvelous?"

Marvelous? Try fucking unhinged. I shake my head, a humorless chuckle escaping my throat. "You've really outdone yourself this time, Mother. Breaking into my home, violating my privacy, trying to force me into...into...this twisted breeding program? That's low, even for you."

Her eyes flash, all pretense of maternal warmth vanishing in an instant. "Mind your tongue, boy. You forget who you're speaking to."

"Oh, I know exactly who I'm speaking to," I shoot back, my voice cold and cutting. "A manipulative, controlling bitch who can't handle the fact that I won't dance to her sick little tune anymore."

Amethyst flinches at my language, but I ignore her. She's just another pawn in this fucked up game. My mother, though...she looks ready to breathe fire.

"How dare you," she hisses, her composure cracking like brittle ice. "I have given you everything - wealth, power, status. And this is how you repay me? By throwing it all away for some gold-digging slut?"

That's it. The final straw. I'm in her face before I can blink, my finger jabbing into her chest, my vision tunneling with rage.

"You shut your goddamn mouth. Cara is worth a thousand of you, a million. She's the best fucking thing that's ever happened to me, and I'll be damned if I let you sully her name with your poison."

I'm dimly aware of movement in my peripheral - the good doctor slowly backing away, Amethyst's wide-eyed stare. But all I can focus on is the icy fury etched into every line of my mother's face.

"You're making a mistake, Juniper," she warns, her voice low and lethal. "A mistake you'll regret for the rest of your miserable life."

"No," I say, my voice so deadly-soft it could cut through steel. "I will not be your pawn, your prized stud horse for breeding. I don't care about the money, or the empire. I care about her - the woman I love, the woman I've wronged in so many ways but who still owns every beat of my fucking heart."

I square my shoulders, meeting my mother's frigid gaze with a fire of my own. "Disown me, disinherit me, I don't give a single flying fuck anymore. I choose her. I choose Cara. And I will spend the rest of my goddamn life making this right, earning back her trust, loving her the way she deserves to be loved."

In the stunned silence that follows, I feel a weight lift from my chest. A lightness I haven't known in years, maybe ever. The shackles of the Deveaux name, the expectations and manipulations, they fall away like rusted chains.

I am free. Finally, utterly free.

Ignoring the sputtering protests of my mother, the wide-eyed shock on Amethyst's face, I stride towards the door. The bodyguards tense, ready for confrontation, but I simply smirk.

"Oh, I'm leaving, boys. And if any of you even thinks of stopping me, just remember - I'm a Deveaux. And we always get what we want."

But he remains unmoved.

"I'm afraid I can't let you leave, sir," the lead goon says, his voice a monotone rumble. "Mrs. Deveaux's orders."

I bark out a laugh, the sound harsh and jagged in the charged air. "Of course. Can't have her prized stud escaping the breeding program, can she?"

I take a step forward, then another, until I'm nose to nose with the human barricade. "Listen carefully, because I fucking despise repeating myself. You have two choices here. You can step aside and let me pass, or I can make you. And trust me, you don't want option two."

They're well-trained, I'll give them that. But they're nothing compared to the fury, the righteous anger coursing through my veins. The seconds tick by, taut and tense.

Freedom, redemption, Cara...they're so close I can almost taste them on the tip of my tongue.

But before I can cross the threshold, my mother's voice cracks through the air like a whip, stopping me dead in my tracks.

"Not so fast, Juniper."

I turn slowly, every muscle tensed for a fight. She stands there, arms crossed, a cold, calculating smile playing at the edges of her lips.

"You didn't really think I'd let you walk out of here, did you?" she asks, her voice dripping with false sweetness. "Not when there's so much at stake."

I grit my teeth, my hands curling into fists at my sides. "I told you, Mother. I'm done playing your sick games. I'm leaving, and there's not a damn thing you can do to stop me."

But even as the words leave my mouth, I feel a flicker of doubt. Because this is Elaine fucking Deveaux, and she always, always has a trick up her designer sleeve.

"Oh, but there is," she says, her smile widening into a Cheshire grin. "You see, darling boy, you have two choices here. You can either cooperate, provide the necessary...contribution...to ensure the Deveaux legacy continues. Or..."

She pauses, letting the silence stretch out like a garrote. I feel my stomach drop, a cold, creeping dread slithering up my spine.

"Or you'll never leave this penthouse again. And you'll certainly never see that little tart of yours. What was her name again? Cara?"

Red. All I see is fucking red. I lunge forward, ready to wrap my hands around her throat, to squeeze until the poisonous words stop spilling from her lips. But before I can reach her, the goons are on me, restraining me with iron grips.

"You fucking bitch," I snarl, straining against their hold. "You can't do this. You can't keep me here against my will."

Mother just laughs, a cold, tinkling sound that sets my teeth on edge. "Can't I? I'm Elaine Deveaux, darling. I can do anything I want. And right now, I want my grandchild. The next heir to the Deveaux empire."

She nods at the doctor, who's been watching the whole exchange with wide, fearful eyes. "Prepare the extraction, Dr. Volkner. It seems we'll be doing this the hard way."

Panic rises in my throat like bile. This can't be happening. This can't be fucking real. I thrash against the grip of the goons, but it's useless. They're too strong, too many.

"Mother, please," I beg, hating the weakness in my voice but unable to hold it back. "Don't do this. I'm your son, for fuck's sake."

For a moment, just a moment, I think I see a flicker of doubt in her eyes. A hint of the mother I once knew, the one who sang me lullabies and kissed my scraped knees. But then it's gone, replaced by a hardness, a cruelty I've become all too familiar with.

"You stopped being my son the moment you chose that gold-digging whore over your family," she hisses, each word a twist of the knife in my gut. "Now, you're nothing more than a means to an end. A necessary sacrifice for the greater good of the Deveaux name."

I feel the fight drain out of me, replaced by a cold, creeping numbness. Is this it, then? The end of the line, the final nail in the coffin of the man I used to be?

I close my eyes, Cara's face swimming behind my lids. Her smile, her laugh, the way her eyes sparked with mischief and love in equal measure. She was my everything, my reason for breathing, for being.

And now, because of my own fucked up choices, my own weakness, I'll never see her again. I'll never get the chance to make things right, to be the man she deserves.

I'm dimly aware of being dragged away, of Amethyst's stricken face, the doctor's stammered apologies. None of it matters. None of it compares to the loss, the yawning void that's opened up in my chest, threatening to swallow me whole.

They strap me down, hook me up to machines that beep and whir and invade. Tear away every last shred of my autonomy, my humanity. And all the while, my mother watches, a cold, triumphant smile on her lips.

"This is for the best, Juniper," she says, her voice distant, distorted. "You'll see. One day, you'll thank me for this."

I want to laugh, to rage, to scream until my throat is raw and bleeding. But I can't. I'm trapped, helpless, a prisoner in my own body and mind.

As the sedative takes hold, dragging me down into the waiting dark, I cling to one last thought, one final lifeline in the storm.

Cara. My Cara Mia. The love of my miserable fucking life.

I'm sorry, baby. I'm so fucking sorry. For everything.

Please, don't forget me. Don't let this break you. You're stronger than you know, stronger than I ever was.

Live, Cara. Live for both of us.

I love you.

Always.

And then, oblivion claims me, and I know no more.

Chapter 19
Cara

The rich aroma of freshly brewed coffee usually comforts me like a warm hug, but today the intoxicating scent has the opposite effect. Tendrils of nausea slither up my throat as I stare at the haunting animation playing on my computer screen. It's my latest creation, far darker than my typical whimsical style—elongated, distorted shadows loom ominously, skeletal fingers twisted into claws reaching out from sinister shapes. A perfect manifestation of the inner turmoil devouring me.

"Geez, Cara, you okay?" Louis's familiar voice cuts through the oppressive silence cloaking my studio.

I can't meet his concerned gaze, shoulders hunching inward as the weight of my torment presses down like a crushing avalanche. How could I begin to explain the inky poison leeching into every sun-dappled dream until it corrodes into a waking nightmare?

"Your Instagram's blowing up," Louis prods gently, closing the distance between us to grip my arm. The warmth of his calloused palm has always grounded me before when I felt untethered, but today it's like a flickering candle struggling against the suffocating black void threatening to extinguish it. "Followers are flooding my DMs worried about you after that disturbing animation. Talk to me, bella."

My lips twist in a mirthless facsimile of a smile as I finally drag my gaze up to meet his summer-sky eyes. The tender concern blazing there is like a white-hot lash, searing me with its poignancy. If only for a few crystalline moments, I was blissfully oblivious to the harsh realities calcifying around me.

"Just trying something edgy and new," I rasp out, the lie feeling like jagged shards grinding my soul into shattered dust motes as it passes my lips.

Louis sucks in a sharp breath, strong jaw clenching as his grip tightens incrementally on my bicep. I can practically see the realization dawning, the sickening knowledge that something has gone horribly, irrevocably awry in my world. This is no mere artistic exploration into the macabre, no ironic foray into darkness just for novelty's sake.

This is the desperate scream of a soul being inexorably consumed by the very night terrors meant only to torment, never breach reality.

"Talk to me, Cara." It's half-plea, half-command etched in granite as his piercing gaze bores into mine. "Don't shut me out with empty deflections when I can practically taste the despair radiating off you in waves."

Louis always did have an uncanny gift for seeing past the myriad intricate masks I deploy to shield myself from the world's cruelties. Even now, as fresh horrors sluice through my veins with every panicked beat of my heart, one soul-searing look from him is enough to dismantle decades worth of practiced self-preservation.

The fantasy shatters like a rock delicately tossed through a kaleidoscopic window. In its place remains only the jagged shrapnel of distilled reality—ugly, stark, utterly visceral in its gaping anguish.

Squeezing my eyes shut, I let the dam burst in one cataclysmic deluge.

"The paranoia...the fear of being watched and followed...the lingerie disappearing piece by piece..." I have to pause, swallowing hard against the scalding bramble of tears clawing at the back of my throat as fresh mortification paints my cheeks in lurid stripes. "I think—no, I know—it's all connected to June. And I don't know what to do or how to make it stop."

Louis goes rigid beside me, the reassuring warmth of his solid frame turning to chiseled marble as the harrowing truth reverberates between us in concussive waves. For one interminable heartbeat, all that exists in the universe is the strained rasp of my ruined voice managing the unfathomable: "Has June...has he truly become my tormentor?"

That single damning question unlocks the sluice holding back a virulent tide of long-suppressed emotions. A strangled noise rips free from Louis's lips as his hands fall away from me as if my very presence is corrosive.

"No," he rasps, anguish carving deep grooves in his striking features as he staggers back a step. "Oh god, please don't let it be him doing this. Not June. Anyone but that twisted son of a bitch."

He shakes his head rapidly, agitated hands raking through his overlong chestnut waves in mute denial of the reality slamming into us both with meteor force and irreparable intensity.

Hysteria bubbles up my throat in a frantic giggle edged with incipient madness, the sound seeming to come from someplace outside of my own shattering psyche. "I wish I knew for sure. But there are too many coincidences and red flags pointing back at the man I love—loved?—to keep burying my head in the sand," I whisper, the soft timbre doing nothing to mask the seismic shift rocking my very foundations.

Louis looks as if he's been sucker punched, the breath leaving him in a harsh wheeze. His normally whiskey-warm eyes are blown wide, entire countenance suffused with abject horror. "Cara..."

But I'm already shaking my head, plowing forward with the momentum of a scream ripping itself from the marrow of my bones. "I have to talk to him, Louis. Learn the truth, whatever the cost. It's the only way I'll breathe again."

My voice drops to a caustic rasp as flayed confessions escalate into a crescendo neither of us can deny any longer. "What if my deepest fears prove true? What if denial has blinded me to being the ultimate fool? What if the love of my life is the nightmare entity engulfing me?"

Silence rings like a death knell in the wake of my keening outburst, the words hovering in the arid stillness between us with the potency of forbidden blasphemies given corporeal form. We stare at each other across an unseen chasm of gaping bewilderment and inchoate denial—two souls trapped in a cosmic scale Shakespearean tragedy where betrayal is merely the opening salvo in a downward spiral of pathos, anguish, and inevitable destruction.

I'm the first to fracture, spiderweb fissures renting the rictus facsimile of composure etched onto my face with all the depth of a hollow porcelain doll. Splinters of my fragmented self lacerate flesh and bone as I violently expel them in purging waves, making space for the roiling wasteland of misery and fear metastasizing within.

At some point, Louis's arms enfold me, his body a steadying ballast amidst my undoing. I flail against him, fists pummeling his solid chest as raw, primal screams rent the air. Still he holds me fast, a silent comrade weathering the tempest and letting it spend itself against his ramparts.

After an eternity compressed into a single anguished breath, the maelstrom subsides into jagged, hiccuping breaths. I sag bonelessly into Louis's embrace, words a luxury I no longer possess beyond wheezing gulps of air into constricted lungs.

Slowly, with infinite tenderness, Louis lowers us both until we're kneeling amid the shrapnel of our fractured realities. I curl into his shelter, tethering my frayed consciousness to the steady thrum of his heartbeat as chaos screams in white static behind my eyelids. His strong fingers card through my disheveled hair, lips brushing my brow in an indelible benediction.

"I'm right here, bella," he murmurs, the depth of his timbre resonating down to my marrow. "No matter how dark the storm gets, I'll be your anchor. I swear it on my life."

There will be more moments like this, I know with a fatalistic certainty that feels as old as the cosmos itself. More outpourings of devastation and terror, more incandescent rage and soul-scouring grief once we finally wrest the awful truth into immutable existence. More keening, more rending wails scraped raw from our very quintessence until we imagine we'll never breathe without agony again.

But for this single crystalline moment frozen in amber, I allow my psyche to float untethered as Louis's solidity moors me to shore once more. The torrent has receded for now, nothing but the detritus of our shared cataclysm strewn in its wake.

One way or another, the answers I fear more than oblivion will be exhumed. The sinister whispers and dark forebodings loosed upon my life will claw their way into the immolating light of revelation.

When that day comes, when the shroud obscuring the monster in our midst rends away to expose the full horror of its grotesquery...

I can only pray the unleashed inferno doesn't immolate us all until nothing remains but smoldering ash and the poignant echoes of unrealized dreams.

After all, some truths are more perilous to confront than any mortal mind can truly prepare for once freed into harsh reality.

We tumble out of the theater in a rowdy pack, the stale stench of fake butter and overpriced snack fodder clinging to our clothes like a miasma. I'm still buzzing off an adrenaline high from the cinematic gore-fest, rattling off the most gloriously fucked up kill sequences with grisly glee.

"That wood chipper scene was epically vile!" Song crows, dragging his hands through his mop of hair like he's trying to physically scrub the memory from his brain. "But also, like, insanely impressive from a technical perspective? Those practical effects were next-level seamless."

Sonya scoffs at his transparent attempt to varnish his perving with an artsy critique. "Please, you were too busy drooling over the naked chick getting slashed in the shower to properly appreciate the nuances."

Before Song can fire back with his typical dudebro protests about objectivity and enjoying cinema as a consummate art form, we're interrupted by a familiar figure materializing out of the crowd.

Alex, looking like they'd rather be anywhere else, is trying to blend into the crowd. Keyword: trying.

"Alex!" I call out, waving them over with a forced grin. "Fancy seeing you here!"

They approach reluctantly, shoulders hunched and eyes darting around like a cornered animal. "Hey, Cara. Fancy that." Their voice is strained, the usual easy charm notably absent.

"You've been avoiding me," I state bluntly, crossing my arms. "Spill. What's going on?"

Alex shifts uncomfortably, running a hand through their artfully tousled hair. "Look, Cara, it's not you. It's just..." They trail off, gaze skittering away from mine.

Understanding clicks into place with sickening clarity. "It's June, isn't it?" I ask, voice flat and brittle. "He's been scaring off my dates."

The guilty flush staining Alex's cheeks is all the confirmation I need. White-hot fury lances through me, warring with a traitorous curl of perverse satisfaction. The twisted, primal part of me revels in the idea of June wanting me so desperately, so completely, that he'd resort to such underhanded tactics.

Song lets out a low whistle, shaking his head. "Damn, sis. Your man is hardcore."

"That's some real alpha male romance novel shit," Sonya chimes in, a wicked gleam in her eye. "Possessive, obsessive, borderline unhinged..."

"The perfect book boyfriend!" they chorus together, dissolving into giggles.

Even Mom can't quite hide her smirk, though she tries to school her features into a disapproving frown. "Now, now, you two. That kind of behavior is hardly appropriate in real life."

I know they're right, know that I should be appalled and outraged by June's actions. But a small, secret part of me thrills at the notion of being so utterly, consumingly desired. The kind of passion that transcends reason and propriety, that burns with the intensity of a thousand suns.

The kind of love story that rivals the most epic of romances, the most heart-wrenching of happily ever afters.

Shaking my head, I try to dislodge the dangerous train of thought. "You're right, Mom. Twisted shit like that is best left to the pages of my favorite guilty pleasure reads."

But even as the words leave my lips, I can't quite extinguish the embers of longing smoldering in my chest. The traitorous whisper that maybe, just maybe, June's brand of all-consuming devotion is exactly what I've been craving all along.

Alex clears their throat, drawing me back to the present. "Anyway, I just wanted to let you know what's been going on. I didn't feel right keeping it from you."

I nod, mustering a strained smile. "Thanks, Alex. I appreciate you telling me."

We exchange a few more awkward pleasantries before parting ways, the weight of June's specter hanging heavy between us. As we make our way to the car, Sonya bumps her shoulder against mine, a knowing glint in her eye.

"You know, as fucked up as it is, there's something kind of hot about a guy being that crazy about you," she muses, voice pitched low so only I can hear. "I mean, don't get me wrong, it's totally toxic and problematic. But still..."

I snort, shoving her playfully. "You're incorrigible, you know that?"

But even as I roll my eyes, I can't help the tiny thrill that zips down my spine at her words. The forbidden allure of being someone's entire world, their reason for breathing.

It's a dangerous game, toying with the idea of June's obsession. A Pandora's box I know I shouldn't even contemplate opening. But as we pile into the car, laughter and good-natured ribbing filling the air, I can't quite shake the niggling sense that maybe, just maybe, I'm already in too deep to turn back now.

After all, every epic love story needs its fair share of drama and angst, right? The push and pull, the will-they-won't-they, the all-consuming fire that threatens to burn everything in its wake.

Maybe June and I are just acting out our roles in the grand saga of our own twisted happily ever after. Maybe his brand of madness is the key to unlocking the passion I've been so desperately seeking.

Or maybe I'm just fooling myself, grasping at straws to justify the unjustifiable.

Only time will tell which way our story will unfold. But one thing's for certain—I'm in for one hell of a ride.

Chapter 20
June

The silence presses in on me, a physical weight bearing down on my skull. I pace the length of my cage masquerading as a penthouse, the plush carpet doing little to muffle the manic energy thrumming under my skin.

Bruises mottle my skin, my breaths coming in shallow rasps. The taste of copper lingers on my tongue. But it's not the physical blows wracking my body that leave me shattered. No, it's the memories that refuse to grant me reprieve.

Mother's voice, dripping poison honey. "You will do your duty, Juniper. As a Deveaux heir." Amethyst's coy touches, her expectant looks that feel like sandpaper grating against my raw nerves. The phantom warmth of Cara in my arms, now nothing more than a haunting spectre.

I grasp my phone, thumb hovering over Judith's contact. She's the only lifeline I have left in this godforsaken family. But even as I press the call button, shame curdles in my gut. What kind of man am I, relying on my sister to fight my battles?

"June?" Judith's voice crackles through the speaker, concern lacing her tone. "Are you okay?"

A bark of laughter rips from my throat, jagged and humorless. "No, Jude. I'm not. I haven't been for a long time."

Silence, then a soft sigh. "Talk to me, little brother. What's going on?"

The dam breaks, everything flooding forward in a torrent of anguish. Mother's machinations, her relentless pressure for me to fall in line, marry Amethyst, play the dutiful son. How she's taken over my home, my life, stripping away any illusion of control.

But it's more than that. It's the insidious poison she's been dripping into my ear for years, warping my sense of self, my understanding of love. The way she's weaponized my fears, my insecurities, molding me into a twisted reflection of her own desires.

"She's killing me, Jude," I rasp, my voice splintering under the weight of revelation. "Slowly, painfully. Erasing everything that makes me human, everything that makes me yours brother."

Judith's sharp inhale echoes through the line, a mirror of my own realized horror. "June," she breathes, a world of understanding in that single utterance. "What do you need me to do?"

Relief crashes through me, so intense it steals my breath. "I need you to create a diversion. Something big enough to draw Mother's attention, just for a little while. So I can slip away, see Cara."

A beat of silence, then, "Consider it done. When should I—"

"Now," I interrupt, the urgency clawing at my throat. "It has to be now, Jude. I can't spend another second in this gilded torture chamber."

"Okay," she says simply, resolve hardening her tone. "Go. I'll keep her occupied for as long as I can."

"Thank you," I breathe, the words wholly inadequate. "For everything. I love you, Jude."

"I love you too, little brother. Now go get your girl."

The line goes dead and I spring into action, a man possessed. I throw on a hoodie and jeans, a laughably ineffective disguise, but the best I can manage with my meager options.

My heart pounds a staccato beat against my ribs as I crack open the penthouse door, peering into the hallway. Empty, thank fuck. Mother's watchdogs must be occupied with whatever chaos Judith has undoubtedly unleashed.

I slip out, every nerve ending alight with tense anticipation. The elevator ride down is an eternity, each passing floor a countdown to freedom or damnation.

When the doors finally slide open, revealing the gleaming lobby, I half expect an army of guards to descend upon me. But there's only the doorman, eyeing me with bored disinterest.

I step out into the crisp night air and it's like a vice around my lungs eases, allowing me to breathe fully for the first time in weeks.

Now, to find Cara.

I hail a cab in a daze, mumbling her address in a fever pitch. The car can't move fast enough, the city blurring past in a smear of neon and shadow. Adrenaline courses through my veins, a heady cocktail of fear and determination.

All too soon and yet not soon enough, we pull up to her building. I practically throw a wad of bills at the driver, stumbling out on unsteady legs.

My feet carry me to her door, muscle memory overriding the haze of panic. I knock, a harsh, staccato rhythm that pulses in time with my thundering heart.

The moment stretches, an agonizing limbo. Then the lock clicks and the door swings open, revealing Cara's face. Shock, then confusion flickers across her features, her gaze roving over my disheveled appearance.

"June?" My name is a question on her tongue, colored with trepidation and the faintest hint of hope. "What are you doing here?"

"Cara," I breathe, the word reverent, desperate. "I had to see you. I had to—"

But the words die on my tongue as her eyes widen, fear and concern bleeding into her expression. "Oh my god, your face. What happened?"

It's only then I remember the mottled patchwork of bruises painting my skin, the blood crusted at the corner of my mouth. Mementos of my failed escape attempts, of Mother's increasingly physical efforts to keep me under her thumb.

Cara's hands flutter about me, delicate fingers ghosting over each purpled mare. Her touch is a balm and a firebrand, soothing and searing in equal measure.

"It's nothing," I rasp, catching her wrist gently. "Nothing, compared to being away from you."

Her throat bobs, lips parting on a soft exhale. "June, you can't just show up like this. Not after everything."

"I know," I say, a broken whisper. "I know I've fucked everything up, that I've hurt you in ways I can't even begin to atone for. But Cara..."

I swallow past the lump in my throat, vision blurring with the threat of tears. "I can't do this without you. Can't be the man I need to be, the man I *want* to be, if you're not by my side."

A shuddering breath escapes her, the glimmer of moisture in her eyes mirroring my own. For a moment, we simply stare at each other, a conversation passing between us in the silence.

Then, with a barely audible "come in," she steps back, allowing me entrance.

I follow her into the apartment, the familiar scent and sounds of her enveloping me like a long-lost embrace. The door closes softly behind us, a period at the end of one chapter, a promise of a new beginning.

Cara turns to face me, arms wrapped tight around her middle. A protective instinct surges through me, fierce and unyielding. I long to gather her close, to shield her from the world, from the poison I've allowed to seep into the cracks of our foundation.

But I hold back, sensing her need for space, for control. She draws a fortifying breath, the words visibly forming on her tongue.

"June, we need to talk about—"

But I cut her off, unable to bear the thought of rehashing my sins, of picking at the scabs of our fractured bond. "Can we just...can we have tonight?"

My voice cracks, raw and bleeding. "One night, to just be June and Cara. To forget the world outside that door exists. Please, sweetheart. I'm begging you."

Conflict wars across her face, the battle between self-preservation and longing. It's excruciating, watching her weigh the decision to open herself up to me once again, knowing I'm the one who planted those seeds of doubt.

"Please," I whisper again, the word a broken litany. "I need you."

Something in her expression shifts, crumbles. With a muted noise somewhere between a whimper and a moan, she surges forward, claiming my mouth in a bruising kiss.

I meet her with equal desperation, fingers tangling in her hair, pulling her impossibly closer. It's messy and graceless, more a violent collision of need than a tender embrace.

Cara presses against me, all soft curves and shifting muscle. She licks into my mouth, a hot slide of tongue that sends bolts of liquid fire straight to my core. Her hands slip beneath my shirt, nails scoring paths of delicious possession along my ribs.

I walk us back towards the bedroom, unwilling to relinquish even an inch of contact. We fall to the mattress in a tangle of limbs, the springs creaking in protest.

Clothes are shed with fumbling urgency, a trail of fabric breadcrumbs mapping our frenzied journey. When she finally writhes beneath me, bare and flushed and perfect, it's like coming home and witnessing the divine in a single stolen moment.

"June," she gasps as I lavish attention on the column of her throat, teeth and tongue painting abstract devotionals into her skin. "Please."

I answer her plea with action, fingers tracing arcane patterns along the sensitive flesh of her inner thighs. When I finally, tortuously breach her sodden folds, her back arches clean off the bed, a primal moan torn from her lips.

I work her mercilessly, stoking the flames of her rapture with the kind of single minded focus I usually reserve for atonement. She is my altar and I, her penitent worshiper, determined to prove my devotion with each flick of my tongue, each curl of my fingers.

Cara shatters on a choked sob, my name a broken hallelujah as she clenches rhythmically around my digits. I coax her through the aftershocks with reverent caresses, each tremor a benediction.

When she finally stills, chest heaving, I crawl up her body to claim her mouth once more. She licks her essence from my lips with a decadent hum, the vibration shivering across my nerve endings.

Rolling us over, Cara straddles my hips, a wicked gleam in her eyes. "My turn," she purrs, a delicious promise and implicit threat rolled into one.

She takes me into the wet silk of her mouth without preamble, the sudden envelopment ripping a guttural groan from my chest. My hands fist in her hair, fighting the urge to thrust into the tight suction of her throat.

Every stroke of her tongue, every rhythmic hollowing of her cheeks drags me closer to the edge of bliss. When she takes me to the hilt, nose buried in the wiry thatch at the base of my cock, my vision whites out, a howl of ecstasy shattering the heated silence.

But she pulls off before I can find my release, a petulant whine escaping me at the loss. Crawling up my body with feline grace, she positions herself above my straining arousal, a Cheshire grin curling her kiss-swollen lips.

"Tell me you want me," she demands, eyes dark and glittering with unbridled hunger.

"Fuck, Cara," I pant, the words a desperate rasp. "I want you. I need you. Please, love. Don't make me beg."

She hums, a considering sound, even as she notches the thick head of my shaft against her dripping entrance. "You beg so pretty," she muses, a sultry tease. "But I suppose you've been a good boy tonight."

Then, with a sinuous roll of her hips, she sheathes me to the hilt.

I let out an animal noise, fingertips digging into her hips with bruising force as she rides me with single-minded abandon. It's fast and dirty, a frantic coupling infused with every unspoken fear and desperate hope.

As she clenches around me, her breathy moans a siren's song in my ear, every nerve in my body pulls taut, coiling in anticipation of cataclysmic release. I bury my face in her neck, losing myself in her scent, her softness, the slick slide of her body against mine.

For a few precious, stolen moments, there is only this. Only us, moving together, chasing oblivion and salvation between rumpled sheets. The world beyond these four walls fades away, inconsequential. Unreal.

But as she shudders above me, my name a broken curse on her tongue as we tumble over the precipice together, reality seeps back in, casting its long shadows across our afterglow.

Rolling off me with a satisfied sigh, Cara pillows her head on my sweat-slick chest. I run my fingers through her tangled locks, brushing a reverent kiss against her temple.

"I love you, Caramia," I murmur, the words slipping out unbidden. "No matter what happens, no matter what I've done...that will always be true."

She stiffens almost imperceptibly, the post-coital haze evaporating like mist beneath the harsh light of day. Propping herself up on one elbow, she fixes me with a searching gaze, the vulnerability in her eyes a knife to my gut.

"Then why, June?" The question is a ragged whisper, barely audible above the erratic thundering of my pulse. "Why did you do it? The lies, the manipulation...stalking me?"

And there it is, the poison apple at the core of our fractured fairy tale. The truth she deserves, the confession I've been choking on for months.

I close my eyes, steeling myself against the revulsion, the betrayal I know will color her features. Drawing a shuddering breath, I force the words past the knot in my throat.

"Because I was afraid." A broken admission, each syllable drenched in regret. "Afraid of losing you, of not being enough. Of being the kind of man my father was, the kind of man my mother wanted me to be."

I open my eyes, meeting her gaze head on, refusing to shy away from the judgment, the disgust I know I deserve. "But in trying to hold onto you, to keep you safe...I became the very thing I feared. A monster, twisted by my own insecurities and poisonous upbringing."

Tears spill down her cheeks, each one a glittering accusation. The sight rips into me, flaying me open and exposing every rotten, putrid piece of my soul.

"I'm sorry, Cara," I rasp, my own vision blurring. "I'm so fucking sorry. I know I don't deserve your forgiveness. I know I've broken us in ways that might never be mended."

Reaching out with trembling fingers, I cup her cheek, half expecting her to flinch away. But she leans into the touch, a reflexive seek of comfort, even now.

"But I swear to you, on everything I hold dear…I will spend the rest of my days trying to be worthy of your love. Of your trust. Even if it takes a lifetime, even if you never look at me the same way again…I will never stop fighting to be the man you deserve."

Her lip trembles, a fragile, crumpled thing. "I want to believe you, June. God, I want to. But how can I trust anything you say, after everything you've done?"

And that's the crux of it, isn't it? The poison I've allowed to seep into the very foundation of our love, eroding it from the inside out.

"You can't," I whisper, the admission brutally honest. "Not yet. Not until I prove it to you, with every action, every choice. Not until I become someone…something…worthy of your faith once more."

Untangling myself from her reluctantly, I stand, harsh fluorescent light throwing my myriad sins into stark relief. Crossing the room with heavy, determined strides, I reach for the first instrument of my betrayal.

My hands shake as I reach for the first camera, nausea climbing up my throat. I have to do this. Have to slay these demons, purge this poison before it seeps out and taints Cara beyond salvation.

But even as I work, unhooking each instrument of violation with trembling fingers, regret rises like bile. What have I done? How can I possibly atone for this betrayal?

"June?"

Cara's voice slices through my spiraling thoughts. Her eyes flicker from my face to the camera clenched in my white-knuckled grip. Horror dawns, a slow, sickening crawl.

"You..." She falters, realization settling like a stone. Confusion, disbelief, a maelstrom swirling across her features. Then, devastating in its finality, betrayal.

The camera slips from my hand, a resounding thud in the suffocating quiet. "Cara, let me explain—"

"Explain?" The word comes out strangled, raw. Her voice climbs, edged in hysteria. "Explain what, June? That you've been spying on me this whole time? That I can't even trust my own home anymore?"

I reach for her, desperate to bridge this chasm rending open between us. She flinches back as if my touch burns. "Cara, please. I was trying to protect you, to keep you safe."

She bares her teeth, a fractured, humorless sound tearing from her throat. "Safe? You put cameras in my home. You violated my privacy, my trust. You made me feel crazy for suspecting it."

Tears spill down her face, saltwater trails carving through any composure. The sight is a blade between my ribs, knowing I'm the cause of her anguish.

"I'm sorry," I rasp, the apology like shards of glass on my tongue. "I'm so fucking sorry. I never meant to hurt you."

"But you did." Her voice splinters, knees giving out as she sinks to the floor. "You destroyed us, June. You took something precious and twisted it into something ugly."

My own tears fall free, each one an inadequate penance for the suffering I've wrought. I crouch down, aching to gather her in my arms even as I know I've forsaken any right.

"I know I fucked up," I whisper, hoarse and cracking. "I know I've lost myself. But Cara, my love for you, it's the one thing that's real. The one thing that's kept me breathing."

She shakes her head, a fractured denial. Her eyes, once so warm and bright, now shutter, closing me out.

"I want to believe you," she says, a dead, hollow note in her voice. "I want to believe that this isn't who you are. That the June I fell in love with is still in there somewhere."

She draws a shuddering breath, steeling herself. Then, devastating in its quiet resignation, "But I don't know if I can ever trust you again. Not after this."

Striding over to the bed, I sink to my knees before her, a penitent at the altar of her judgment. Grasping her hands in mine, I press fervent kisses to her knuckles, each one a wordless vow.

"I'm yours, Cara Mia," I breathe against her skin. "Mind, body, and soul. To cherish, to worship, to serve…for as long as you'll have me. And even if you cast me out, even if you never want to see my face again…I will love you until my dying breath."

Pulling her hands from my grasp, Cara gasps, a choked, broken sound.

"I think you should go," she whispers, each word a razored edge. "I can't…I can't do this."

I stand, every muscle screaming in protest. The urge to fight, to fall to my knees and beg, surges through me. But I tamp it down, the last scrap of clarity telling me to respect her wishes. To grant her this, even as it rips me to shreds.

"I'll go," I manage, voice a mangled wreck. "But Cara, this isn't over. I won't give up on us. On you."

A ghost of a smile flits across her lips, there and gone. "I know you won't." A whispered confession, an absolution I don't deserve. "But right now, I have to give up on you. Even if it kills me."

And with those words, she walks away. The soft click of the bedroom door is a gunshot, a shattering.

I stand amidst the ruins of our love, the cameras a damning jury at my feet. The weight of my sins presses down, threatening to drive me to my knees.

I will make this right. I will claw my way out of this abyss, drag myself through the flames of purification. I will become a man worthy of her love, her trust, even if it takes a lifetime.

This isn't the end of our story. It's the crucible, the trial by fire that will forge me anew.

And when I emerge, tempered and cleansed, I will find my way back to her. Back to the light.

No matter the cost.

Chapter 21
Cara

The world tilts on its axis, a sickening lurch that sends reality skittering out of focus. I stare at the cameras, neat little soldiers of betrayal lined up on my dresser, and it's like I'm watching a stranger's life unravel.

This can't be real. It can't be.

But it is. The truth of it crashes over me in relentless, pummeling waves. June, my June, the man I trusted with every fractured piece of my soul…he did this. He violated my privacy, my sanctuary, in the most ruthless way imaginable.

Bile rises in my throat, hot and acrid. I swallow it down, but the taste lingers, a tangible manifestation of the revulsion churning in my gut. My skin crawls with phantom sensations, the prickling awareness of unseen eyes tracking my every move.

How long? How fucking long has he been watching me, a voyeur in my most intimate moments? The thought sends a shudder rippling through me, a full-body revulsion I feel in my marrow.

"Cara…"

June's voice reaches me as if from a great distance, muffled and distorted by the roaring in my ears. I flinch away from his outstretched hand, a visceral recoil I can't control. He lets it drop back to his side, a broken puppet with cut strings.

"Don't." The word cracks like a whip, harsher than I intend. "Don't you fucking touch me."

Hurt flashes across his face, quickly replaced by a resigned sort of anguish. "I'm sorry, Cara. God, I'm so sorry. I never meant for you to find out like this, I never meant to hurt you—"

A jagged laugh rips from my throat, a sound more akin to a sob. "Hurt me? June, you shattered me. You took the trust I placed in you and ground it to dust under your heel."

My voice splinters, tears blurring my vision. I blink them away furiously, refusing to grant him the satisfaction of seeing me crumble. But inside, in the secret, shadowed corners of my heart, I'm bleeding out.

Because even now, even in the face of this unforgivable betrayal...a traitorous part of me yearns for him. For the comfort of his arms, the steadiness of his presence. It's a sickness, this love, an addiction I can't seem to shake no matter how hard I try.

That realization, that hidden kernel of weakness, ignites a spark of fury in my chest. It burns through the fog of shock, the haze of despair, until I'm vibrating with it. With the sheer, unadulterated rage of a woman scorned.

"Get out."

The words hang between us, a razor's edge. June flinches, raw devastation etching into the lines of his face. "Cara, please. Let me explain, let me—"

"I said get out!" I don't recognize my own voice, twisted and seething with a vitriol that frightens me. "Now, June. Before I call the fucking cops and have you arrested for invasion of privacy."

His eyes widen, fear and disbelief warring across his features. "You wouldn't."

I lift my chin, a silent challenge. "Try me."

We stare at each other for a charged, awful moment, the ruins of our love scattered at our feet. I can see the moment he realizes I'm serious, that there's no salvaging this, no pretty words that can bandage the hemorrhaging wounds.

Slowly, as if the very act is physical agony, he turns to leave. At the threshold, he pauses, throwing one last, shattered look over his shoulder. "I never stopped loving you, Cara Mia. Not for one second. I hope one day...one day you can believe that."

The soft click of the door closing behind him is a gunshot, a gavel strike. I stand motionless, frozen in the wreckage of my life, until I hear his car start up, the sound fading into the distance.

Only then do I allow myself to break.

Sobs wrack my body, great, heaving things that claw their way up from some primal, agonized place deep in my chest. I'm drowning in it, in the tar-thick misery that coats my lungs, chokes my breath.

Through the haze of grief, one coherent thought crystallizes.

Sonya. I need Sonya.

Scrabbling for my phone with trembling fingers, I dial her number. She picks up on the first ring, as if she's been waiting for this call all along.

"Cara? What's wrong?" Her voice is sleep-rough but immediately alert, concern thrumming through each word. "Are you okay?"

"No." It comes out as a strangled croak, barely recognizable. "Sonya, I need you. Can you...can you come over? Please?"

"I'll be there in ten." There's rustling in the background, the jingle of keys. "Just hang on, okay? I'm on my way."

I don't remember hanging up, don't remember sinking to the floor. All I know is the cold press of hardwood against my bare legs, the way my lungs strain for air that won't come.

Time slips sideways, unspools in fits and starts. It could be hours or heartbeats before I hear the key turning in the lock, the quick, light tread of Sonya's steps.

Then she's there, dropping to her knees and pulling me into her arms without a word. I collapse into her, boneless, a marionette with cut strings. Violent, wrenching sobs shake me, staining the soft cotton of her shirt with saltwater.

"Oh, Cara," she murmurs, rocking me gently. "Oh, honey. I'm so sorry. I'm here, I'm here."

I don't know how long we stay like that, curled around each other in the dimness of my living room. Eventually, the tears subside, leaving me wrung out and aching. Sonya eases back, smoothing sweat-damp hair from my face with gentle fingers.

"What happened, sweet pea?" she asks softly, though I suspect she already knows. My sister's always been intuitive like that, attuned to my turbulent emotional currents.

Haltingly, in fits and starts, I tell her. The words feel like broken glass in my throat, slicing me open from the inside. Sonya listens without comment, though I can feel the tension thrumming through her, the barely restrained urge to find June and rip him apart with her bare hands.

When I finish, she's quiet for a long, considering moment. Then, with a soft sigh, she presses a tender kiss to my forehead.

"I'm not going to insult you by saying everything's going to be okay," she murmurs, her lips brushing my skin. "Because right now, I know it feels like your world is ending. Like you'll never be whole again."

I make a small, hurt sound, burrowing deeper into her embrace. She tightens her arms around me, a silent promise.

"But I will say this, Cara Briers. You are the strongest, most resilient woman I know. You have weathered storms that would break lesser people, and you've come out the other side every single time."

She pulls back, framing my face with her hands. Her eyes, so like my own, blaze with a fierce, protective love.

"This is going to hurt like hell. It's going to feel like dying, like every breath is a battle. But you will survive this. We will get you through this, no matter how long it takes. You hear me?"

Tears well anew, but this time, they're tinged with something like hope. A fragile, flickering thing, but present nonetheless.

"I hear you," I whisper, my voice a ragged wisp. "I don't…I don't know how, but I hear you."

Sonya nods, a small, sad smile playing at the corners of her lips. "One day at a time, sweet pea. One hour, one minute if that's what it takes. We'll be here, every step of the way."

I sag against her, suddenly exhausted. The events of the past few days crash over me like a tsunami, leaving me flayed open and drowning.

Sonya, attuned to my every shift as always, rises to her feet, pulling me up with her. "C'mon, let's get you to bed. Everything else can wait until morning."

I let her lead me to the bedroom, too drained to protest. She tucks me in like she did when we were kids, smoothing the covers with a tender hand.

As she turns to leave, a sudden, irrational surge of panic seizes me. My hand shoots out, grasping her wrist with clumsy desperation.

"Stay," I plead, not caring how pathetic I sound. "Please, Sonya. I can't…I don't want to be alone."

Her expression softens, an aching tenderness smoothing the worried lines of her face. "Of course, Cici. Scoot over."

She climbs into bed beside me, curling around my back like a protective parenthesis. The steady thrum of her heartbeat against my spine is a lullaby, a tether to reality in the churning tempest of my mind.

Exhaustion drags at me, a bone-deep weariness that no amount of sleep can touch. As I hover on the precipice of unconsciousness, lulled by my sister's even breathing, a sudden memory lances through me.

The nausea. The dizziness. The way my body has felt like a foreign thing, betraying me in subtle, inexplicable ways.

No.

The thought is a whiplash, a bucket of ice water dumped over my head. Surely the universe isn't that cruel, that capriciously vicious. There has to be another explanation, another reason for the insistent curl of dread in my gut.

But even as I scramble for alternative explanations, the truth sinks in with sickening certainty. A hysterical laugh bubbles up my throat, escaping in a strangled little gasp.

Pregnant. I'm fucking pregnant.

Sonya stirs against my back, an inquisitive hum vibrating through my skin. "Car? What's wrong?"

For a moment, I consider laughing it off, shoving the horrible revelation into the shadows of my mind. But I can't carry this alone, this anvil-weight of terrible knowledge.

Slowly, I twist in her arms until we're face to face. In the gloom of the bedroom, her eyes are depthless pools, filled with a concern so raw it steals my breath.

"I think I'm pregnant," I whisper, the words like nails in my mouth. "I think...God, Sonya. I'm pregnant with June's baby."

The breath rushes from her lungs in a sharp exhale, a punch of surprise. She's silent for a long, terrible moment, the gears of her mind visibly turning behind her eyes.

When she finally speaks, her voice is a careful, studied neutral. "Okay," she says slowly, evenly. "Okay. Have you taken a test?"

I shake my head, mute. The thought of peeing on a stick, of seeing my fate confirmed in stark pink and white, makes my gorge rise.

Sonya nods, as if I've given her an answer anyway. "Right. Okay. That's step one, then. We'll get a test tomorrow, and we'll go from there."

"Go where, Sonya?" My voice cracks, splinters. "Where can I possibly go from here? I'm carrying the child of the man who violated my trust, who ripped my heart to shreds. What am I supposed to do?"

Tears carve hot, bitter trails down my face. I feel unmoored, cast adrift in a storm-tossed sea with no land in sight.

Sonya pulls me close, tucking my head beneath her chin. I burrow into her warmth, desperate for any scrap of comfort, any fleeting sense of safety.

"I know it feels impossible right now," she murmurs, her voice a soothing hum against the shell of my ear. "I know you're scared, and angry, and hurting in ways I can't even begin to imagine. But Cara, you're not alone in this. No matter what happens, no matter what you decide...I'm here. We're all here. You don't have to face this by yourself."

A sob hitches in my throat, gratitude and despair warring in my chest. "I don't know what to do, Sonny. I don't know how to be a mother, how to raise a child alone. And June..."

The name is a blade between my ribs, a piercing ache that steals my breath. Sonya rubs soothing circles on my back, a steady comfort in the whirlwind of my thoughts.

"You don't have to decide anything tonight," she soothes, a gentle reassurance. "Let's just take this one step at a time, okay? Tomorrow, we'll get a test and go from there. Everything else can wait."

I nod against her collarbone, too wrung out to argue. She's right, even if every fiber of my being screams in protest. I can't make any earth-shattering decisions in the throes of heartbreak and blind panic.

So I let my sister's steady presence lull me, let the cadence of her heart drum a fragile staccato of peace against my ribs. Tomorrow, the cold reality of my situation will crash over me anew, an inescapable tide.

But for tonight, for these scant few hours before dawn...I rest. I breathe. I cling to the only lifeline I have left in the wreckage of my upended world.

Soon I drift off, tumbling into the dark honey of sleep. There are no dreams, no respite from the nightmare my life has become. Just a yawning void, an abyss of unconsciousness I gladly sink into.

But even in the depths of my slumber, one thought persists, a glowing ember in the smothering black.

Pregnant.

It could almost be funny, in a bleak, humorless way. Like a cruel punchline to a joke I'm not privy to.

Pregnant, by the man who shattered me.

Pregnant, facing the most monumental decision of my life.

Pregnant, and utterly, inescapably alone.

My last thought before I succumb to the waiting dark is a grim, inescapable truth, a fact that will color every waking moment from here on out.

No matter what I decide, no matter what impossible choice I make...my life will never be the same. The girl I was, the woman I thought I'd grow to be...she's gone, ashes scattered on the unforgiving wind.

In her place stands a stranger, a husk of my former self. A broken simulacrum navigating an alien landscape with no map, no guiding star.

Just the fragile, fluttering heartbeat beneath my own. A promise and a curse, a tiny seed of impossible potential amidst the salted earth of my ruined world.

Pregnant.

God help me.

About the author

Fortuna Lux is a real-life queen of steam, an unapologetic provocateur spinning wickedly erotic tales for readers who crave love stories with a dark and daring edge. Drawing on her own experiences as an adventurous woman navigating the complex world of desire, Fortuna isn't afraid to push buttons and boundaries in her work. Her specialty is serving up dominant, dangerous heroes and the strong, sensual heroines who bring them to their knees.

When she's not dreaming up sizzling new stories, Fortuna can be found savoring a well-aged whiskey, practicing her rope skills on her submissive, and amassing an army of houseplants. She believes in fearless exploration, both on and off the page, and loves connecting with fellow romance rebels who share her passion for all things kinky and unconventional.

Also by

Novels

Canvas of Our Souls

Obsessed: A BWWM Body Worship BDSM Story

Coming Soon

Ruthless Desire

Say You're Mine (Book 2 of the Shattered Hearts Duet)

Made in the USA
Middletown, DE
09 July 2024